Drew's life sucks. Saving money to escape his homophobic family is one thing, but his only paying gig at the moment is playing his father's "only gay in the village" plus-one to every LGBT friendly business event.

Then his brother comes up with a plan. Sheffield needs someone to go undercover for his police investigation. Drew has all the qualifications: he's gay, he has experience with exotic animals, and he's college-aged. And he's easily bought.

Going undercover to solve the mystery of a college campus smuggling ring was never in his plans. Neither was hot, perfect, house captain Rylee. The inside jokes about cats, animal prints, and talk of a place called Vihaan that forbids same-sex relationships, are just the tip of the suspicious iceberg.

Little does Drew know that he's about to expose more than an illegal smuggling operation. The truth could be more lethal than he could imagine. And, despite it all, it might be his own secret past that kills him before the truth can be unveiled.

A Touch of

Danger

Surviving Vihaan

Elaine White

A NineStar Press Publication

Published by NineStar Press
P.O. Box 91792,
Albuquerque, New Mexico, 87199 USA.
www.ninestarpress.com

A Touch of Danger

Printed in the USA
First Edition
February, 2020

Print ISBN: 978-1-951880-44-6

Also available in eBook, ISBN: 978-1-951880-43-9

Warning: This book contains sexually explicit content, which may only be suitable for mature readers, reference to a past rape, past trauma, physical and mental abuse, domestic abuse, drug use, and homophobic slurs.

Chapter One

"Care to run it by me again?" Drew rubbed his jaw, trying to stifle his laughter while his brother prowled the small office.

"We think they're smuggling exotic animals," Sheffield explained, with a drawn-out sigh.

"Through a fraternity house?"

"Yes." His brother glared, as though *he* was the crazy one for questioning this "case" he'd been asked to consult on.

Drew took a slow, steady breath and asked, "You know this, how?" He was trying not to sound judgemental, but he wasn't buying this story. What the hell would a bunch of fraternity brothers want with exotic animals? He paused...the idea conjured uncomfortable images. He hoped there was no "bear pit" with the animals or dubious sexual practices. He had a weak stomach and didn't want any part of *that* kind of investigation.

Still, his brother was the big bad cop in the family. Drew was the runt; the unworthy second son. Abandoned to do whatever he wanted with his life because he was already a disappointment. There wasn't much he could do to lower his position in the family. But he was no cop, no action man, and no Sherlock Holmes. He knew nothing about solving a case or how to look for evidence of "foul play". And he was allergic to certain animals.

"We've had reports of wild animals on the grounds. When we sent an officer to investigate, he was attacked by a large cat. When we tried to run the names and identities of those living in the house, we came up with nothing. These people don't exist," Sheffield explained, shaking his head as he paced the length of the tiny room. "We sent in another man, undercover, to grab whatever DNA he could get his hands on. What he brought back...well, the hair came back feline. Exotic cats—a panther, a lion, and a cheetah."

Now Drew was getting the heebie-jeebies. He wasn't sure he wanted anything to do with exotic cats. He wasn't allergic to cats, which meant he would need to try harder to wiggle out of this. "I'm not a cop." And this was getting weirder by the second.

"No, which will work for us. The last few cops we've sent in undercover have been caught quickly. These guys are smart and professional." The heavy stare Sheffield levelled made Drew want to shrink. But he wasn't a five-year-old anymore. "*You* are a college kid looking for somewhere to belong. It will be tough. They're private and secretive. They barely socialise outside their group of friends, and they don't date outside the house."

"Seriously?" Raising his hands, Drew asked for a pause as he considered those words. This job went beyond weird and into the downright kinky. "You mean—"

Sheffield nodded, a grin spreading across his lips. "They're gay, bi or trans. They call themselves the LGBT House of Acceptance," he revealed. Arching an amused eyebrow while pretending not to find it hilarious.

"Nice name," Drew scoffed, knowing what Sheffield was implying.

"This isn't anything to laugh about. These guys are serious illegal traders, and we need to shut them down," he argued. The growl could have been funny if it wasn't for the fact he was being used.

"Let me get this straight, brother of mine. You suggested me for this because I'm gay, right?" he asked, getting straight to the point.

"It helps."

"Yeah. You! It won't help me much."

Sheffield waved off his concerns and sneered in his usual dismissive manner. "You're a hermit. This will be good for you," he claimed.

Drew knew he didn't give a shit whether it was good for him. Sheffield was like their dad—he thought being gay was a choice Drew made when he turned sixteen and came out to the family. A choice made to piss off everyone and gain attention because the almighty big brother had been accepted into the Police Academy. Fuck them. He wasn't as narcissistic as his family.

"I happen to like being a hermit."

"Will you do it? Because I need to tell my supervisor, and then we need to fit you for a wire. You'll be going in tonight." Sheffield stopped his pacing to level Drew with an intimidating stare which hadn't worked since he was ten.

Nothing like short notice.

"No wire," he decided.

"Excuse me?" He growled—fucking growled!—and Drew wanted badly to do a fist pump, in victory.

"You said these guys are smart? Professional? They'll spot a wire. They'll probably cavity search me," he teased, wiggling his eyebrows. Sheffield was practically pimping his brother out to criminals. Not like he'd turn down a good frisking if the company was good-looking. "Let me handle it. I'll get your evidence and report back in a week. This Saturday."

Hell, he was being paid. He'd dress in a monkey suit and do the hula if they asked. Maybe he could use the cash to get out of this shit hole?

Sheffield raked both hands through his short dark hair. "The boss won't like this," he complained, in a quiet, unsure voice.

Rising from his seat, Drew tried hard not to smile. "Yeah, well he's not done a great job so far, has he? We'll try it my way, and, if it doesn't work, we'll do it your way," he offered.

He was going to get what he could out of this. Out of this town and well away from his family. Sheffield was bearable in small doses, but the rest of his family were vipers snapping at his heels. Each one determined to ignore and berate him when he needed them. Ready to jump on board and use him for their own means when they needed a boost.

Doing this, for a bit of cash, was like when he'd attended an LGBT fundraiser with his dad a year ago, in return for a year's worth of college tuition. As long as it got him away from his family, he had no dignity and no pride.

Not a shred.

Chapter Two

Walking up to the fraternity house, Drew removed his phone from his pocket and switched it off. He didn't want Sheffield or his supervisor hacking into his phone, somehow turning the recording function on. Whatever happened tonight, he would do his job, but he'd do it his way.

The front doors stood shut, but enough music seeped through the cracks to let Drew figure out the beat if not the words. Taking a deep breath, he climbed the four steps to the front door and knocked.

According to Sheffield, the house wasn't open to visitors or parties not organised by the Captain of the House, Rylee. He was taking a chance by showing up uninvited. With a duffel over his shoulder and a story to get him in the door, he waited.

The man who opened the door was nearly six-foot, with short but shaggy dirty blond hair. He had the most captivating dark brown eyes he'd ever seen, with a flicker of red which was probably a trick of the light. Gorgeous didn't come close to describing him. "Well, look what the cat dragged in," he said, with a quirk of a smile. His words playful, with a sexy undertone. The mention of a cat didn't escape Drew's notice either.

"More like kicked out," Drew admitted, starting his cover story right off the bat. It wasn't far from the truth. His family had kicked him out. Attending an LGBT fundraiser with his dad, for good publicity, had eased the way back in. "I heard this was the place to come if I needed a place to stay on short notice."

The man at the door watched Drew, guarded. "According to who?"

He shrugged and grabbed the strap of his bag in both hands. "Rumours. No one in particular." Drew knew better than to name names. Sheffield hadn't said who to blame for the information he had about the fraternity house. "If they were wrong, I can leave. I need to know before it gets too late," he said, as he glanced around the darkening campus grounds. He'd timed his visit to look like he'd been thrown out by his parents when they got home from work and had come straight here. It was late enough most people wouldn't open their doors if he had to go anywhere else.

"The rumours are true," the man admitted, taking a step back and leaving the door open. "You can stay the night, but there will be conditions if you want to stay any longer."

Drew nodded. "Sure. I can look for somewhere else tomorrow. Thanks." He stepped inside, passing by the tall man much closer than he would have liked.

A quick sniff from the blond's direction had him unnerved, but he tried not to react. He kept going, further into the main hallway, then stopped. He waited to discover where he could bed down for the night.

"I'm Rylee," the man said, holding his hand out.

"Drew." He grasped the hand in a quick shake and watched Rylee closely. His blue eyes met brown, and a shiver crept up his spine. The Captain of the House was evaluating him, unwilling to release his hand. "Can I have my hand back?" Drew asked, flashing a smile to make it seem like a joke.

Rylee cocked his head and tugged his hand until Drew stumbled into his broad chest with a yelp of surprise. Rylee dipped his head and sniffed Drew's chocolate brown hair, in the weirdest "hello" he'd ever had. "You seem nervous. And scared," he pointed out.

"Yeah, well...I *have* been kicked out of my parents' house and have nowhere to live. I think I have every right to be scared." Drew's voice showed his frustration, though his body screamed with curiosity. And a strange attraction to this odd, blunt man. "I'm now homeless and broke. Whoopie for me." Forcing his hand out of Rylee's grip, he gestured to the stairs straight ahead of the front door. "Want to show me where I'll be sleeping tonight?"

Rylee's serious look morphed into a grin. He waved Drew forwards and said, "Follow me, and I'll find you a bunk."

Drew followed and evaluated everything he could see as they climbed the fifteen steps. From the animal artwork on the walls to the animal prints on the fabrics, he got a good idea what the house was famed for. At the top of the stairs, a few bedrooms extended along the corridor towards the front of the house. Most extended to the corridor directly to the right, with only one straight ahead. "I'm guessing you guys are real animal lovers?" He nodded towards the nearest room.

Rylee chuckled and gave Drew's back a gentle push towards the room on the far end of the long hallway. "An inside joke," he claimed, completely avoiding the subject. He opened a door and gestured for Drew to go inside.

Drew laughed it off, choosing not to make a big deal out of it while casting an eye around the room. Compact, clean, simple. He was a few steps from walking into the daybed pressed against the right-hand wall and assumed the door ajar on the other side led to a bathroom. A nice perk. The double bed against the far wall was likely Rylee's, with a wardrobe and dresser. The rest of the room was dedicated to an intense study area, a desk buried under a mountain of books and stationery.

"This is my room, but I keep a bunk for any strays who walk in on dark nights," he chuckled, crossing to the bed under the window.

Drew tried to ignore his words, which constantly referenced animals. "Any rules I need to know about?"

Rylee perched on the edge of his bed, while Drew unpacked a wash bag from his duffel. "Don't disrespect others. Don't expect anyone else to clean up after you. Don't disrespect boundaries or press a conversation when it's clearly not wanted. No intimate touches, as some couples here are open while others are territorial."

There he went again with the animal references. "No problem. I'm single and not on the lookout for any complications in my life," he promised. The last thing he needed was to fall for another liar or cheater. He'd had his fill of both.

Eyeing him carefully, Rylee began an unnerving barrage of questions that shook Drew's composure. "Are you willing to skip classes if necessary?" he added, with a glare implying *necessary* was a substitute for *if I told you to.*

"If it's important," Drew agreed, figuring this was a test to see if he was suited to their exotic animals export business. If he could make sure he was suitable, they might bring him in on their next trade and give him the information he needed.

"Are you allergic to animals?"

"Dogs, mostly. Horses, rabbits and fish, oddly enough."

"Do you like animals?"

"Sure. Everything but house cats. They're evil little bastards."

Rylee laughed, letting his gaze drift a little further south than Drew liked. This guy was hot, big and full of muscles, the type to get his heart racing and his dick jumping for attention. But he'd been there, done that and had the physical and mental scars to prove it. He wasn't going to fall for it again. "Can you care for others before yourself?" he asked, still smiling.

Drew frowned, not liking his tone. "I'm not a selfish asshole." He wondered if he could ask this Rylee guy to answer the same questions. "I give money and food to the homeless when I can. If a roommate is sick or is going to miss classes, I'll help out any way I can."

"Good. I think we'll get along fine." Rylee gave a nod, suggesting Drew had passed whatever weird test he'd given. "Out of curiosity, what do you prefer I call you? Are you gay, straight, bi, trans, or nonbinary? What are your pronouns?" Rylee asked, once again throwing too many questions at once.

Drew was glad he'd asked. He had a Female-To-Male friend who bravely battled the ignorance of their friends. Ignorant asses who continued to call him by his birth name, Rebecca. No one could accept him as Beck. "You can call me Drew. I'm gay and a "he". You?" he asked, intrigued to find out more about this stunning specimen of a man. Not like he'd show his attraction, but there was no harm in looking and imagining.

"The same, "he". And very gay," Rylee replied.

Drew couldn't help but snort, sure this guy was a regular charmer. Dangerous enough to convince him to stay far, far away.

"Well, it's late. Take the bathroom first and get ready for bed." With the order given, Rylee stood and crossed to the wardrobe.

Drew took a breath, overwhelmed by how quickly it happened. He'd slumped into Sheffield's office at the unholy hour of eight o'clock, to spend most of the day reading his case-files and enduring his charming company. He thought this would be harder, but he wouldn't argue against an early night. At least he had a bed and warmth; he hated to imagine the case if he'd been in the predicament his story indicated.

Grabbing his wash bag and a pair of loose joggers, he headed into the en suite to grab a shower and get ready for a decent night's sleep. His mind whirled with possibilities; why Rylee had been flirting, if he could be the ringleader of an exotic animal smuggling ring. Why a frat house needed the money from an illegal operation, and how they managed to get hold of such animals.

By the time he left the bathroom and sank onto his bed to dry his hair, he wasn't close to answering any of those questions. He avoided looking at Rylee, as he rose from his bed and disappeared into the bathroom. The man was a distraction he didn't need.

Discarding his towel into a laundry basket by the door, Drew headed for bed. He lay with his head at the bathroom end to keep an eye on the door. Contemplating the many ways he could find answers without getting caught.

He needed to question the most gullible frat brother, which definitely wasn't Rylee. Find new evidence of animals within the grounds, if he could. A whisker of an animal reported as stolen could close Sheffield's case.

Ten minutes into his plans, the bathroom door opened. Drew turned onto his left side and faced the wall he hadn't noticed had a huge mural of a wildlife savannah. Everything from elephants, lions, and gazelles painted in incredible detail across the landscape.

These guys didn't know how to keep a secret.

Shutting his eyes tight, he ignored the footsteps of Rylee returning to his bed. If Rylee thought it was weird he'd fallen asleep quickly, he said nothing. Drew could act exhausted tomorrow or claim he'd travelled far after leaving his parents' house. He'd think of something plausible.

He waited for the inevitable goodnight or question of whether he was asleep yet. Fingers drifted over his hair, forcing him to focus on presenting a believable sleeping figure. He'd tried to fake it when he was young, but his dad always knew he wasn't asleep. He'd learned well since then to steady his breathing and relax his face.

"You're beautiful," Rylee whispered. "Beautiful but completely unaware of what you are. We'll take care of you and bring you home, where you belong." Those fingers trailed down his right cheek, fluttering over the pulse in his neck. "Home with me."

Drew's heart rate accelerated at the intimate touch from Rylee. His breath was unsteady even after Rylee removed his hand, footsteps padding the carpet as he walked away.

What the hell?

He hadn't expected anyone to show interest, particularly on his first night. But he definitely hadn't thought anyone would try to make a claim on him. Home with Rylee?

Tempted to roll over and ask, pretending to be groggy, a sharp intake of breath made Drew stop. The sound captured his curiosity. He made a sleepy moan and rolled over to face the room. He'd spotted a mirror beside the door able to give him a glimpse of Rylee's bed.

When his movements drew no attention, Drew peeked his eyes open and almost gasped in shock. Rylee lay in his bed, stark fucking naked, the sheets thrown back. He wore not a stitch of clothing and tugged mercilessly at the sizeable cock in his hand. A faint growling escaped him as his hips bucked off the bed.

Drew knew he should look away, but he couldn't. This was for him. Wasn't that what Rylee meant when he said Drew's home was with him? The guy thought he belonged here. It wasn't wrong to watch a strong hand gripping his long dick, drawing the foreskin to allow his thumb to brush the slit of his head, was it? Hell, it was a thing of beauty, done in his honour. He had a right to look, didn't he?

The problem was he didn't want to look. He hadn't had sex in two years since the last asshole cheated on him and left him with a black eye, three scratches, and a broken nose. Since then, Drew hadn't been able to trust any man who was bigger than him.

Rylee, most definitely, was bigger. In the right ways.

Licking his lips, he couldn't resist the urge. Reaching under the covers, Drew palmed his cock through his joggers, biting his lip to stop from moaning aloud. On the second nudge, his fingers catching the head to draw it up and give it a good grope, he stopped breathing.

In the reflection of the mirror, Rylee met his gaze and roared as he shot a stream of come over his chest. He never broke eye contact, as he trailed his fingertips over his chest, sweeping up his come, and licked his fingers clean.

It was one of the hottest things he'd ever seen.

"Goodnight, Drew." His rough, orgasm-filled voice dragged Drew straight into his own spiral. He curled in and tried not to scream through one of the strongest orgasms he'd had in years.

Holy fuck!

Rubbing his face against his pillow, he tried to remember why he was here. Not to be fucked by the biggest, roughest piece of tight abs and big cock he could find. Nope. Not his mission.

Damn, if he didn't wish it was.

Chapter Three

Drew woke, relieved he'd tiptoed into the bathroom around one o'clock to wash and change his joggers. He didn't enjoy waking sticky from a solo venture. His teen days of suffering through those mornings were long over.

Still, it was disheartening but relieving to wake and see Rylee wasn't in the room. His bed smelled like sex, but Drew tried not to notice. He focused on his morning ritual of shower, brush teeth, comb hair, do stretches and get dressed. Once done, he padded downstairs in his bare feet, a pair of joggers loose on his hips and a T-shirt keeping him covered in company.

He wasn't sure if Rylee would mention what had happened last night or if he'd already told the other frat brothers. Passing through the large living room full of animal prints, Drew kept his eyes open. Gorgeous framed photos of the Serengeti, a plush sofa, and three huge La-Z-Boy armchairs, filled the space. He tried not to let the comfy surroundings matter. Not every nice home was hiding a dark secret.

The living room led into the dining room with no more than an archway, opening to a space twice as big as the living room. Drew noticed no one at the dining table, fit to seat twenty, seemed surprised to see him.

"Drew! Welcome." A tall blond man approached with a warm smile, holding his arms out in greeting. Embracing him in a tight hug before he had a chance to back away. "We're happy to offer you sanctuary as long as you need it." The words were formal, welcoming, and a little weird.Drew had never been embraced into anyone's life. Wriggling out of the hug, he flashed a weak smile and waved to the group of ten guys sitting around the dining table.

"I'm Lorcan. Let me introduce you to the boys," he insisted, guiding Drew closer to the table. Except, he didn't want to get too friendly with these people. They were criminals and he was here to put them in jail. "Sitting at the head of the table, I'm sure you recognise Rylee."

Drew almost cringed when Rylee winked, his gaze drifting low while Lorcan rattled off a dozen more names. He couldn't concentrate with such attention on him. Rylee hadn't even been in his seat when he first looked, his T-shirt sweaty enough to imply a form of morning exercise. How did the man appear during the length of one hug?

He ignored the naming ceremony and nodded whenever one of the guys offered a smile or wave in response to their introduction. When it was over, Lorcan gestured to the seat kitty-corner from Rylee. "Nice to meet you," Drew said, knowing their names didn't matter. He was the new guy and could use the whole "not great with names" excuse later.

Rylee grabbed a plate and placed it at Drew's spot, filling it with sausages, waffles, beans and bacon. "You eat meat, right?" he checked, though it was a little late if he didn't since his plate was full of the stuff.

"Yeah," he replied, grabbing his knife and fork. He moved half of the six sausages, two of the five pieces of bacon and two of the three waffles onto Rylee's plate, which was already full of food. "I'm not a total pig. I'd like to be able to move when I'm finished."

A few chuckles followed his words, though he was far from joking. He ignored them to begin eating, aware of Rylee watching from the sidelines. He didn't once complain about the food Drew had landed on his already loaded plate. He ate slowly, never taking his eyes off Drew.

It was unnerving.

"Drew," Lorcan said, still as eager and chirpy, "are you currently enrolled or signing on to classes? I looked for your name on the register and couldn't find it. I was going to mark your transfer to the house on your records." Lorcan was an early bird too. Like Rylee and his need for a pre-breakfast run. Fine. More work for him.

Swallowing, Drew relaxed with his forearms resting on the edge of the table, his knife and fork poised over his plate. "I'm registered as Andrew," he explained, rolling his eyes at the truth. "My dad is a stuffed shirt who can't trust me to find my own dick without help. He enrolled me under my given name as a "fuck you" to the biggest disappointment in the family."

Lorcan's eyes grew wide, but Rylee chuffed at his side.

"I'm pretty sure you found your dick fine, last night," Rylee muttered. If it wasn't for a few sniggers Drew would have hoped no one else noticed.

Glaring at the bigmouthed bastard, he snapped, "I may be a worthless little faggot, but I can find my dick fine. I have a degree in animal psychology, specialising in felines. I've studied animal bereavement counselling and modifying animal aggression. I've volunteered at a zoo, rehoming exotic animals, and was in charge of the breeding program for the big cats. I've done more in my twenty-five years of life than my useless piece of shit father has done in fifty years. I'm. Not. Dumb."

That was why he was here. He was the only person Sheffield knew who had any experience with wild and exotic animals. He was perfect for the job, minus the badge.

Rylee raised an eyebrow, but it was Lorcan who sighed and spoke.

"Drew," he said, waiting patiently for his attention. He had his hand on top of another; the guy sitting next to him, who flushed and stared at his plate. "You're new here and don't know us, which we'd be happy to fix. But please don't use that word in this house. Some of us have bad experiences with it," he hinted, glancing at the guy sitting beside him.

Clearing his throat, Drew gripped his cutlery tighter. "Sorry. I guess I've got a few hang-ups myself," he admitted, shaking his head. His little tirade was hardly likely to endear him to the house. "I'm sorry."

"It's okay," Lorcan replied. He gripped the guy's hand—was it Delaware?—and released him to return to his breakfast. "I can tell you have issues with your father. Most of us have trouble with family, so feel free to share. We understand, in one way or another. It's not easy being who or what we are out in the open."

Who or what? was a strange way to put it but Drew understood.

"Especially in Vihaan." The sigh he released suggested life was hard there. Wherever it was. A tiny little town in the middle of nowhere, probably.

Drew gave a nod, though Rylee glared at Lorcan, who flushed under his gaze. Not knowing what the look meant, he changed the subject. "I've signed on for a law course. My dad insisted. I'll bunk my classes and let him figure it out," he confessed, earning a few more sniggers of recognition. "It doesn't matter how many times I tell him I'm not interested, he can't let go. Why not let him waste his money and support me for a year or two? By then, I'll have a steady job and enough money to escape this shit hole."

"I'm with you," a voice said from his right. The guy was short, ginger-haired and had a sweet, cute face full of freckles. When he caught Drew looking, he flushed a burnt red and ducked his head to eat. "My folks kicked me out, too, a little over a year ago. I have a few months of my course left. The college gave me financial aid to finish. Then I'm out of here," he elaborated, once he swallowed.

Yeah, that was the dream, right? Get Sheffield this big score at work and he was done. Gone.

*

After breakfast, the house held a meeting. Drew stayed for the housing, funding and chores, but cried off when it turned personal. He didn't know these people well enough to eavesdrop on their private lives. No one had an objection, which helped him slip out of the house unseen.

Heading around to the back garden, he sank onto the bench propped against the side of the house. The garden was huge, more than big enough for wild cats to roam if let out to stretch their legs. Plus, the shed at the end of the garden could house cages big enough for exotic pets.

Having worked at the zoo, he knew enough to gauge sizes and needs for the wild cats Sheffield had mentioned. He made the calculations in his head, arriving at a count of four animals at one time.

Wild cats went for a cool sum these days. A clouded leopard was recently sold for five thousand, while a regular leopard was closer to four. The same went for panthers. A snow leopard's pelt could go for eight hundred in the likes of Afghanistan. While a live tiger could earn a little over forty thousand. Photo opportunities, pay-to-play trades and sick fight clubs would buy an exotic animal for a few hours and discard them later.

If these guys had a hand in that, he'd gladly take them down.

"I feel...unstable," a voice said close by.

Drew turned but found nothing but a vent in the side of the house. Intrigued, he slid across the bench, closer to the opening and listened. It sounded like the meeting going on inside.

"My cat is...insistent," Rylee's voice seeped through the cracks. "He's flooding me with feelings I'm not ready to face and I...I don't know what to do. Even running isn't helping to calm him. He's—" He stopped and sighed, sounding at the end of his wits.

It didn't make sense. Having a cat was normal, but claiming it was "flooding" him with feelings sounded weird. Maybe he'd grown attached to one of their products and didn't want to send it away? That would sound logical and tallied with those "do you care about animals" questions. Running. Did that mean his morning run was *with* the cat? Drew had missed an incredible photo opportunity, to prove they at least *had* wild cats on the property.

Now he had to find another way of getting proof.

At least he had confirmation Rylee was a good target. He could use the sizzling attraction between them to get information. First, he had to figure out how hard to push.

Maybe he should let Rylee seduce him?

Chapter Four

The meeting hadn't gone to plan, but Rylee was glad to have gotten things off his chest. He forgot how good it was for the other boys to see him unravel. To show them they weren't the only ones having trouble with control. But he wouldn't let Drew off the hook. He'd cried off the meeting, insisting he didn't know them well enough to hear their private thoughts and problems. Rylee wasn't convinced. He headed to the garden, where he found Drew sitting alone on a bench, staring off into the distance.

"Are you settling in?" he asked, approaching the bench and hovering to find out if Drew was in the mood for company.

"Sure. It's different, but not in a bad way." Drew shrugged and sank further into the seat. Staring ahead as though he saw something important he needed time to fathom out. "I'm not used to going a whole day without a screaming match," he joked, with enough venom Rylee could feel the pain he was hiding behind the humour.

Sitting, Rylee took a deep breath of the crisp air. "You like to deflect with sarcasm, don't you? It's not healthy." He waited to find out what he was thinking and how he'd react to a little innocent questioning. "I'm not prying to know why you do it or what your dad has done to you, but I can see the massive chip on your shoulder. It shoots off rockets every time you open your mouth, in case anyone missed the flashing neon sign," he warned. Intrigued to know if it was intentional or a survival technique he'd learned over time.

"Hello, Mr. Sarcastic. Nice to meet you." Drew saluted him, sitting straight and adopting a straight-laced, stern look. One he dropped quickly while shaking his head in disgust.

Rylee gave him a few minutes to process what he'd said and think it over. "Do you have any friends?"

"What kind of question is that?" he raged, with a glare.

"A curious one," he replied, intrigued to hear his first response was anger and indignation. What had happened to make Drew defensive and bypass the curiosity others had shown to such a question? "It's the question of someone who is wondering why this fraternity house was your first stop last night. Most guys your age have a dozen friends who have sofas," he clarified. Drew hadn't once mentioned friends refusing to let him stay or not having the space. He hadn't even implied he had friends.

"It's a bloody impertinent question of a bigmouthed bastard," Drew disagreed.

Waiting provided no answer. Rylee pushed for one. "Do you?"

"Have any friends? No," he snapped, turning to face him while folding his arms over his chest. "No, I don't have any fucking friends. I don't have a boyfriend, a best friend, a decent family. I have nothing and no one. So the fuck what!"

"Exactly what I thought." Rylee sighed and lifted his right foot onto the edge of the bench, to wrap his arms around his shin. Drew intrigued him, which had been obvious from the start. Something told him the urge to get closer ran deeper than simple curiosity. "Look, we're a family here. We're a little weird and quirky, but we're decent folk. You can stay here as long as you need, whether you attend classes or not. Like you said, if your dad is paying your tuition for the year, you may as well get a place to stay out of it."

Rylee hoped his soft, careful approach allowed Drew to think sensibly. He didn't want the poor guy running off because they'd had less than pleasant words one time. Guys had vanished when they thought Rylee wanted to step in and be their authority figure. He didn't want anything of the sort; he wanted the guys who stayed in their house to be honest—with him *and* themselves.

As much as he liked to give the benefit of the doubt, most people who came to them for shelter or advice played a part. To survive their family, friends, coworkers, or playing the straight guy, trying not to cause waves. It was important to Rylee to break them of those destructive habits before letting them loose on the world again.

As he'd hoped, his words made Drew take a slow, deep breath and release it in the same way. "Yeah." With a dismissive shrug, he scratched his left cheek. "I'm helping my brother with a work project. Once I get paid, I can get a full-time job, get more money under my belt and get out of here," he admitted, reaffirming the promise he'd made this morning.

"Is it bad? This town, I mean." Rylee's heart hurt to know he planned to move on, but it wasn't his place to dictate where Drew went or when. He would like to get to know him better. He had a feeling he could help.

"The town is fine. It's the bloody people who are the problem," he grumbled, shifting, as though the admission made him nervous.

Nodding, Rylee guessed at the real meaning of those words, "Too close to home?"

"Much too close."

"You said you'd studied a lot and you're twenty-five?" Rylee asked, coming upon another interesting thought.

"Why does it matter?"

"Curious."

Drew snorted, as though "curious" was an accusation. "Yeah. I've always loved learning, since I was little. When I left school, I kept going. I spent the next five years studying for my degree, with a few specialist courses," he confessed quietly. "After, I took a year off, travelling around the Highlands, the islands and Ireland. When I got back, things went to shit. My dad wanted me to become a vet since he could call me a 'doctor' in front of his friends."

Interesting.

Rylee couldn't help but notice most of Drew's words held sarcasm, incredulity or mocked his achievements. He showed no pride in what he'd accomplished, no sign of having embraced his thirst for knowledge.

"I bargained with him," Drew scoffed and shook his head. "He'd pay for college for a year while I considered it, and I'd let him use me as the perfect gay son. A puppet to attend events and wave my rainbow flag, to show off how accepting and forward-thinking my father was," he concluded. The bitterness was evident in his voice, but Rylee wouldn't challenge it. Drew was being more honest and open about his life, his hurt and his anger, than he had hoped.

"Is he political? Is that why you had to play the part?"

"An egoist," Drew replied, without any real care for the distinction. "His new boss is a big supporter of LGBT rights. Dad's kissing ass by parading me around," he explained with a smirk and met Rylee's eyes. "Ever heard of 'the only gay in the village'?"

"Of course."

Drew nodded and chuffed a brief, unimpressed laugh. "That's how my dad treats me. I was the black sheep who had to stay hidden, because I was the only *freak* in the village," he clarified, as though it was no different to how his family treated him now. "With his boss, I'm worth something. I've become the token gay guy at his work events, to keep in with the boss. You'd think no one had ever met a gay guy, the way they behave."

Rylee bit down on his bottom lip as an instinct to move closer and draw Drew into his arms arose. The attraction to Drew was physical, for now. But, the more he learned, the more he wanted to protect him from his family. And his own feelings of self-loathing.

Had Drew *ever* been happy? Could Rylee show him how to *be* happy and embrace it?

"It must be...difficult," he acknowledged, not knowing a better word to use.

A soft sigh escaped Drew and he scooted over on the bench to sit closer to Rylee. He lowered his voice to a whisper and asked, "Why are you here?"

"Sorry?"

"Why are you here, questioning me like this?" Drew asked, his eyes hiding more vulnerability than Rylee had anticipated. He'd hoped to catch Drew off guard, affected by the personal slant the house meeting had taken. This was more than he'd hoped for. "What are you studying?" he continued.

Ah. Caught red-handed. Smiling, he confessed, "Psychology."

"And the penny drops. You're trying to psychoanalyse me? Good luck," Drew offered with a huff. He went quiet for a moment, gaze averted, while his index finger tapped against his arm. "Look, I appreciate you taking me in and this 'trying to know the new guy' act you have, but I don't need it. I don't need you poking around inside my head. If there's anywhere else you'd like to poke around, call me. Until then, I'm not up for these heartfelt discussions." He exploded with a stream of words eliminating any opportunity to reply.

Leaving Rylee speechless, as he watched Drew stand and walk away.

Well, their talk had answered more than a few questions.

Rylee remained on the bench, turning over the surprising evaluation he'd made of Drew. He wasn't a sarcastic egoist with no time for anyone else. He was a hurt, vulnerable man who didn't want to get close to others for fear they'd see the pain underneath the façade.

That was a whole other story.

Maybe Drew was more than a pretty face, but it didn't convince Rylee to turn back on his earlier judgement. He couldn't get close to Drew without putting his heart at risk. He'd been down this road, believing someone needed him, ending up used and stomped on, becoming someone he barely recognised. Those feelings belonged in Vihaan and he wasn't going through it again. Not even with Drew, who was about as ideal as a man could get.

Nope. Not this time. He was smarter now.

Chapter Five

God, Rylee was infuriating! Drew hated having someone poking about in his life, thinking they had any right to his thoughts and feelings. Rylee didn't know him. He didn't have the first clue what he went through.

His childhood had been nonexistent, enrolled in every after-school activity possible. Anything to ensure they weren't home often enough to be a burden to their parents. They had to make their way there and home, catching a lift with another kid if he was lucky. It wasn't a summer problem. Wading through snow as big as Drew was tall, waiting for one of his parents to realise he wasn't home yet and collect him. Which would mean Hell had frozen over, blue pigs flew overhead, and he would have been more concerned with surviving the apocalypse than getting home.

His teen years weren't much better. His parents controlled every aspect of his life, from what classes he took, where he went, as well as which girls he dated. Which Drew did, because God help him if he refused.

Drew sank onto the low wall at the front of the house at the bottom of the path. He rubbed his right eye and stared at the blue sky, trying to banish the thought.

It had been hell trying to date girls, with his dad criticising every move. If he didn't hold their hand enough, if he didn't stare longingly at them during a school event. If he glanced at another boy too long, his dad grounded him for three weeks. Needing to invent a convincing excuse to give his latest girlfriend about why he couldn't see the movie she was desperate to see.

Leaving high school had meant freedom. He'd moved out the minute he was old enough and had saved enough money to move in with his latest boyfriend. When he broke up with the girlfriend he'd kept up to the leavers dance a month after they graduated, he told her he was more into her brother than her. Coming out to everyone in his year, who passed on the gossip. The whole town knew by the time he got home. It had been a relief to move out. Not only escaping Sheffield's judgement, his father's control and his mother's constant looks of disapproval and disappointment. It was like he'd been on death row and given a reprieve at the last second. Like he'd been a caged animal for years, finally released and allowed to roam the world for the first time.

His whole life, Drew had been imprisoned for the crime of being his father's son. He'd suffered the mental, emotional, and verbal abuse as long as he could, before breaking out and disappearing. Freedom hadn't lasted long. Without cash and no job offers, he'd had to accept his dad's money to survive.

He'd made a deal with the devil and fallen into this hell hole because of it. Trapped with a guy who was too hot for words, but who was as much a sadist as his father. More concerned with digging through his brain matter for something interesting, Rylee didn't care about him. Why would he? Drew was nothing special, he knew. It didn't hurt any less, but the truth was rarely pain-free.

"Want a smoke?"

Lifting his head, Drew blinked to see one of his frat brothers standing in front of him, holding a packet of cigarettes and a lighter. One of the younger guys. Keon? Without a word, he accepted one of the cigarettes sticking out of the packet and put it to his lips. He leaned in to accept the light, then went back to moping.

Keon took a seat beside him on the wall but didn't say anything. Good. He was done with talking. He was done with a lot of things.

Drew had gone to the event with his dad as a last favour. His year of college was halfway through and the money was in the college tuition fund already. Sheffield had begged him to do this job, because of his background with exotic animals, and he'd been the sucker to fall for it. He'd thought he was wanted, or at least needed. Convinced his years of studying had come in useful to his family. They would recognise his hard work and lay off the attempts to run his life. Now, he could see how wrong he'd been. He'd been manipulated in a new way and was stupid enough to believe it was real. He'd landed here, in a fraternity house where he knew no one, could trust no one and where the Captain was a nosy bastard trying to invade Drew's thoughts.

What fucking luck.

"Has Rylee been doing his psychology gig?" Keon asked, hitting the nail right on the head.

Drew took a drag and lowered the hand holding his cigarette to his knee. He picked at a loose thread on the side of his jeans and ignored the conversation. He wasn't interested in making friends. He didn't want to fool around with Rylee much anymore. He was damned tired. The lying, the scheming, being a pawn. It was exhausting.

"Yeah, I figured." Keon chuffed a laugh and blew out a cloud of smoke. "It's a bit much when he starts, but it gets easier. It's not like he does it on purpose; he's hardwired that way. He lives to help people, even if he can't help himself," he said, continuing the conversation without Drew.

The last part intrigued him. He ventured a guess, "Someone fucked him up, too?"

Keon turned to raise an eyebrow. "I forgot you wouldn't know." He took another drag and held it, letting go with a sense of foreboding. "About four years ago, Rylee was in this intense relationship. He still lived in Vihaan then but was dating this guy who was a lot like him. What you've got to understand is Vihaan isn't accepting of gay relationships. Anyone who lives there, who happens to be gay or bi or trans, has to leave.

"It's not a law or anything," he corrected, catching the words from the tip of Drew's tongue. Smiling, Keon shook his head. "No, it's not a rule. It's something we know and accept from an early age. Vihaan's don't accept this world's view of relationships; believing a person can love, be loved and have sex without being married first. Vihaan's take relationships seriously. If they don't result in offspring, there's no point in two people wasting their time together," he explained.

Drew nodded, his eyebrows raising as he realised what the mysterious Vihaan was. Finally, the clues pieced together and he realised... Vihaan was a cult. This was the place Keon, Lorcan, Rylee and at least Delaware had come from, if not the entire house. They had banded together in this world because they knew and trusted one other. It explained why Delaware had issues, why Rylee was...odd. Maybe even why he was comfortable around the guys here. They were misfits, like him.

"When Rylee came out, it wasn't an issue. He was an important person in Vihaan, and he'd have to marry, no matter what, to produce at least one child as an heir, if not a spare too." Keon shrugged as he took another drag. "Rylee found out his friend was the same—gay and more interested in a loving relationship than a partnership only resulting in children. They began having an affair until his boyfriend announced he was getting married."

"Ouch." Drew frowned at his cigarette, as he realised how painful it must have been. To be in a relationship with a guy which was already forbidden, and discover the guy would rather fit in than love Rylee. Shit.

Keon touched his hand. "Drew, he married Rylee's sister."

"What?"

His smile turned disbelieving, if not bitter. "Yeah. Rylee was devastated. He'd been with his boyfriend for a few years from what I heard. I couldn't say for sure. Lorcan's the only one who knows the whole story," he admitted. "Rylee stayed in Vihaan to see his sister married, as was tradition, then came here. He bought the house, joined the college and a bunch of us joined him," he continued, this time sounding happier.

"You left?" Drew wondered if it was possible. Didn't cults have a stranglehold on their kid's mental states and physical boundaries?

"Oh, it wasn't easy." Keon eyed him carefully. "We had to abandon everything. Our friends, our family...going back. We can come here from Vihaan, but we can't all cross back," he warned, the severity in his voice suggesting bad things happened to anyone who tried. "Rylee's house here on campus is a haven for those who don't fit in in Vihaan. We come here when we escape. Rylee is our counsellor, our confidant, our adviser and helper. He gets us settled into college, if we want, or in jobs, in society. He makes sure we're taken care of."

Yeah, it sounded like Rylee. Always taking care of other people, from what little Drew had seen. It didn't excuse him from the serious fuck-job he'd done on his mental state.

Keon tapped his cigarette and shrugged. "Some respond better than others and stick around. Those who don't, go on to live a new life and put Vihaan out of their mind forever," he admitted quietly. "It's not easy. Vihaan is...a poison. It seeps into your blood and it feels like you'll never escape."

Drew reacted instinctively; he placed his arm around Keon's shoulders and let the younger guy lean into him. "I'm sorry. I guess we're a lot more similar than I thought. Except, I choose to keep going back," he complained, angrier with himself than with having to make the admission.

"It's not a choice if you don't have an alternative," Keon disagreed, tilting his head enough to peek through his eyelashes. "If your choice is to keep communication with your family to survive or put yourself in danger, how much of a choice is it?"

"Sounds like something Rylee would say," Drew argued, not sure if he was impressed or frustrated.

Keon smiled and whispered, "He did say it. To me." After a brief twitch of sadness dimmed his smile, he confessed the rest of the story. "I didn't leave Vihaan, like the others. Escaping means being banished forever. You can't go back. My father sent me here. He chose to let me study in this world and says he trusts me to return home at the end of my course, because I'll finally see the light."

"The light?"

"To show me this world is full of sin and evil. Vihaan is the purity of the world and the one place where I can be happy," Keon revealed, shrugging again. As though he was lost and there was no other way to express his feelings. "At the moment, he's right. Things in Vihaan are simple. You have rules, laws and appropriate behaviours. It *could* change and accept I'm gay, but as long as the current leaders are in charge, it won't happen. My father believes it will, in the future, and I'll be welcome at home," he said, a wistful note in his voice.

Drew contemplated the possibilities if his father accepted his orientation and didn't try to run his life. He may actually get on with his family, be able to settle down and trust in a relationship, repair his relationship with Sheffield. "Would you want that?" he wondered, not sure what his answer would be if Keon asked.

"I don't know." Another shrug showed he was at loose ends. Keon threw his cigarette down and ground it with the toe of his trainer. "It would be nice. Vihaan is...beautiful. It's the place I still call 'home', because my family, my friends...my heart...are still there. I know what I'd be losing if I went back. And I'm not sure if I could bear surrendering the freedom I have here."

"Yeah." The old catch-22.

Doing this job for Sheffield was giving in to his family and doing exactly what they wanted, but it was also an escape. Even if it was temporary or a step towards true freedom, it was progress. What he risked by refusing and doing nothing came down to one word: opportunity. If he'd baulked at this golden opportunity, who knew where he'd be now.

"I mean, evil and darkness exist here," Keon continued, his voice growing distant and thoughtful, "but at least I can choose not to embrace it and accept it into my life. I can never return to Vihaan and accept a woman as my partner. Accept I'm not meant to love or be loved...accept my future is working to the grave in a job I hate to provide for my wife and a dozen kids," he reasoned, sounding sensible.

It was nice to know Keon had his head screwed on straight. He knew his options, the same way Drew did, but he was at the point where he had to make a final choice, and he didn't know what to do. "I hear you, Keon. I'm going through the same dilemma myself," he confessed, as he owed the poor, conflicted guy that much.

"You would have to marry a woman?"

Laughing, Drew answered honestly, "My dad would party like it was nineteen ninety-nine."

They both laughed. Keon heaved a sigh, and he squeezed his shoulders, to let him know he wasn't alone. It wasn't much, but maybe he needed this chance to get it off his chest?

"I guess we've got time left to figure it out," Keon said, a hint of hope entering his voice.

"Yeah...not long enough though."

"No. Not long enough." Lifting his head, his new friend gazed off towards the main campus grounds ahead of the house. "I don't think any amount of time would be long enough for this decision, do you?"

Chapter Six

Two Days Later

Walking into the kitchen in the morning, Drew stifled a yawn and opened the cupboard above the sink to grab the box of cereal. Taking a bowl from the draining rack, he poured the cereal halfway and grabbed the milk from the fridge. The final addition of a spoon took two seconds, then he was able to devour the first spoonful while leaning against the counter.

He had a big day ahead and couldn't afford to delay. The boys had a routine of sitting at the table for meals Drew wasn't used to. He couldn't remember the last time his whole family sat around one table and ate a meal together.

"Morning," Lorcan said, as he walked in and crossed the room to grab the bread from the cupboard beneath the counter. "Not joining us for breakfast?"

"No. I've got work to do," Drew replied, not letting on he was planning to snoop around the fraternity house today. Most of the boys had classes and the few who didn't had planned a bike ride.

Lorcan nodded, hovering with the loaf of bread while Drew ate. "I'm glad you decided to stay more than one night. It can be hard on outsiders to live with us Vihaan natives, especially when they don't know what Vihaan is like. We can be stupid and selfish enough to forget not everyone knows what we're talking about," he explained, his words rushing out, desperate to prevent Drew interrupting.

He had no intention of doing it, but he was intrigued by the first mention of Vihaan since his conversation with Keon two days ago. Drew had noticed how tight-lipped everyone was about their time in Vihaan when he was around, often changing the conversation or choosing their words carefully.

"I hope you haven't been uncomfortable around us," Lorcan continued quietly. "We don't mean to erect this invisible bubble that risks keeping you at a distance. We're not used to having anyone here not from Vihaan."

"I get it," Drew promised, to avoid another apology. "I'm okay. I don't feel left out. I don't mind I'm not one of you. I'm used to it," he admitted, not meaning any insult, though the crestfallen look on Lorcan's face suggested it had been taken. "I'm used to being on my own. I'm relieved there isn't this huge rush to know every detail of my life or for everyone to become my bosom buddy."

"Ah." Lorcan smiled and nodded. "What are your plans for today? Anything interesting? Mani and I are going for a bike ride through the park, if you want to join us?" he offered, looking hopeful.

It was pointless. Drew had work to do and he'd put it off long enough. He'd had to think after his conversations with Rylee and Keon, which had confused him. It had taken a while to get used to the idea of having even partial freedom from his family, for the time he'd be living here and working on Sheffield's investigation. It would be harder to think about what came next—which road he was going to choose.

Hanging out with Keon had helped. They shared a smoke and sat quietly, contemplating life while enjoying the garden or discussing classes.

"I'll probably get in a prelunch workout, then go see the sights. I haven't been to the library and I have reading to do for my classes," he lied, knowing he'd be doing much more. There was a house to study, the bedrooms and a basement he had to search, which could offer a clue to the "cat" secret inside jokes.

Lorcan nodded but didn't seem too interested, as he'd deliberately chosen a boring explanation to keep them off his back. He'd use his phone to document any evidence he found, and if anyone caught him, he could say he'd ducked into the nearest room to take a private call.

Drew had made sure to show a fierce protection of his privacy. He shouldn't be questioned if someone discovered him somewhere he shouldn't be. He could claim he'd heard their approaching footsteps and worried about being overheard.

"Well, I better get started." Drew offered Lorcan a weak smile and put his empty bowl and spoon into the sink, to fill it with water. He liked to let his dishes soak, especially whenever there was something like milk in them. "If you leave your dishes in the sink, I'll get them. You guys are busy today," he said, knowing the offer would be welcome, but would also give him something to do if he required a "cover" story.

"Thanks, that would be great." Lorcan flashed a smile and headed out of the room with the bread. Convinced he was settling in as well as everyone thought he was.

Drew couldn't afford to. If he felt at home here, if he got comfortable, he'd never be able to make the right choice. He had to decide if he was staying to repair things with his family or if he was going to do this job to the best of his abilities and skip town.

Right now, he had no clue.

*

It took an hour for the house to empty, giving Drew enough time to get in a brief work out in his bedroom, walk to the campus library and return to the house. It was easier since he'd scared Rylee away. The guy had gone into hiding since their talk two days ago, which suited him fine.

He began in Rylee's room, since he was the most intriguing of his fraternity brothers. Drew had been flirting in minor levels, on and off over the last few days, to no avail. Rylee showed interest with his eyes, never letting his hands do the talking between them. He didn't even jack off at night to thoughts of him anymore, which had been nice that first night. He'd hoped to find the attraction taking heat, the more time they spent together.

At least if anyone returned for forgotten books, bags or a phone, he'd be in his room.

Drew kept his mobile in his pocket for snapping photos if he needed them for evidence to hand over to Sheffield. Shutting the door behind him, he began rummaging through the dresser drawers, though it contained his own clothes. He wanted to make sure it had no hidden bottoms to the drawers, no false backs or additions to hide secrets from prying eyes. Like his.

Finding nothing in the dresser, he went to the wardrobe beside Rylee's bed and repeated the search. On the top shelf, he found a USB drive which intrigued him. Having no time to explore it, Drew carried it over to his laptop, opened the lid and pressed the On key. As it booted, he left the USB at the side and returned to give the wardrobe a last inspection.

He found a few cat hairs but nothing else.

Drew returned to his laptop, input the password and waited for the desktop to arrange his post-it notes, the calendar and his folders, before plugging in the USB drive. He could look at the contents later. Right now, he copied everything onto a hidden folder on his desktop and removed the drive to put it back where he found it.

Ten minutes later, once he'd searched Rylee's room, Drew moved on and spent a few minutes in each of the other rooms. He found nothing more than animal hairs, suspicious in texture and colour but not enough evidence for Sheffield. They already knew exotic animals were being moved through the house. They didn't need to catalogue the various types.

Drew found accounts ledgers on Lorcan's computer, but a quick phone call to Sheffield proved the police had already discovered them through hacking his computer, during their last undercover op. At least the guy had been good for something, getting them close enough to the computer for a remote hacker to access the files. They had verified the purchases as a legitimate online business. Not eBay, like he'd assumed, but Etsy, the more creative site. According to Sheffield, Lorcan made bracelets, necklaces and sculptures using natural materials, every one with an apt theme of "wild cat". Sheffield called it ironic. Drew didn't have the heart to tell him what ironic meant.

After the bedrooms, Drew spent an hour searching the library from top to bottom. He discovered a few oddly named books about exotic animals and their care, but nothing specific against the house. It was easy enough, living on campus, to claim the books as research for a class.

Once he reached the basement, he sank to perch on an abandoned desk and took a deep breath. If he didn't find anything, it was likely there was nothing to find. He'd searched high and low on a day when no one was there to hinder his search and walked away empty-handed. Surely there was nothing to find, right?

After a few minutes, he rose to his feet and walked around the room. He counted his paces and stopped when he reached the door to the count of ten. It made no sense. Two rooms stood above this, both about seven paces long. Where had the extra four feet gone?

"Hmm, finally something doesn't add up," Drew muttered. Returning to the bottom of the stairs, he counted and took the length of the room as well. That part was fine. He pressed his hand to the far wall and checked every inch for a discrepancy or a door in the wood panelling.

"Come on." He used his fingernails to check for an edge he could get a hold of. After five minutes his nail caught and he found what he'd been looking for. "Bingo!" Drew rushed over to the desk and rummaged through the drawers, stopping when he found a letter opener. It was exactly what he needed to use as leverage against the door.

It took an infuriatingly long time to get it open an inch, and then he was able to use his fingers to pull it open the whole way. Behind it, a four-foot-wide corridor was hidden from view. Even more surprising, when Drew walked in, he looked to the right and left to find it extended the entire length of the room. Along the entire back wall, chains and restraints hung on the wall.

Drew grabbed his phone and took a half dozen photos for evidence. Choosing the share option, he hesitated over adding a name to send the message to. He could think of a million reasons for the chains, one of which an underground BDSM club. Perhaps "cat" was a nickname in uncertain company, used for subs. He didn't see Rylee being sub material; he was a dom, if anything. Was the "cat" he'd complained about a submissive he'd grown too attached to?

Maybe it explained why the guys put Rylee first and looked on him as a leader. Why they flocked here from their little cult, Vihaan.

Second-guessing his discovery, Drew put his phone away. He had to investigate this BDSM possibility, to put his mind at rest. If it turned out to be something completely innocent—well, at least not illegal, since BDSM was far too hot to be innocent—he wouldn't have to regret turning the boys in for something which wasn't a crime. He wouldn't be pointing Sheffield to innocent people, where he'd no doubt do something stupid and reckless.

Right now, Drew needed to be careful. He was beginning to feel at home here and he didn't want to insult anyone or make a mistake. His job for Sheffield was harmless but betraying the trust the boys had offered was unforgivable. It felt wrong to spy on them, never mind double-cross them.

If he got to know Rylee better, it could clarify his feelings and help him figure out what to do.

Chapter Seven

After having lunch and putting in a batch of muffins he'd made from scratch, Drew was no more settled on his plan of action. Baking was the one task, outside academia, to soothe his nerves and help him relax. Reading a short gay romance story hadn't helped, and revisiting the basement for a closer inspection, then gathering various samples of animal hair from the bedrooms hadn't helped either.

Nothing stopped him from thinking about those chains, the hidden room or the frightening thought of Rylee and his fraternity brothers labelled as criminals. They could be nothing more than kinky college boys.

Drew went for a run, leaving his cookies to cool on a rack while he was out. It seemed to do Rylee a world of good every morning. He figured there was no harm in trying.

After ten minutes, frustration set in, as his thoughts swirled, sweat trickled down his spine and his feet ached. It shouldn't be this hard to get his brain to think sensibly and work out a problem. He stopped in his tracks when he spotted Rylee ahead, stopping by a bench to tie his shoelace. Drew had no idea whether to stop and try to draw his attention or whether he should high tail it to the house and get about his business.

"Drew!"

He turned, surprised to find someone other than Rylee approaching. His roommate was still fussing over his trainers, while Drew turned to give Keon his full attention. "Hey, bud." He waved as his new friend approached with a class bag over his shoulder.

"Hey. I was heading for the campus café to get a sneaky doughnut and coffee. Want to come with me?" Keon asked, calm and relaxed for the first time in days. It was great to see since they'd both been struggling with the aftermath of their conversation from days ago.

Drew turned towards the fraternity house and slung an arm around Keon's neck. "Well, if you'd settle for a muffin and my coffee, we can head to the house and have a comfy seat," he suggested, watching Keon's curious frown and the way he stepped in line hesitantly.

"We have muffins?"

"We do now," he informed him. "I bake when I'm stressed, and there was this problem in one of my classes I couldn't fathom. I baked muffins. I'm a sucker for triple chocolate." Drew hated lying, but there wasn't much he could do. He hadn't yet figured out what was best: tell the truth and face the whole house turning on him or maintain the charade and risk losing what he'd found here, regardless.

At least, he supposed, telling the truth meant he'd find out who really cared about him. He'd know who was willing to hear his reasons and who dismissed him as a traitor.

"Triple chocolate?" Keon questioned, with a growing smile.

"Yup."

"Okay. Muffins," he agreed, sounding pleased by the change of plans. "Boy, you're sure learning fast how to earn your keep, huh?"

Drew appreciated the gratitude those words held, suggesting he was giving back with his baking. "I sure am."

*

Drew was leaving the bathroom, after a shower, when he spotted something unusual. It remained hidden unless standing in the bathroom doorway, proven when he stepped into the bedroom or one step into the bathroom to find it was no longer visible.

A single patch of a square crack in the ceiling, which could have been an attic hatch. Wallpapered with a cream, textured paper, it was hard to notice. The seams of the patch disguised by the seam of two strips of paper.

Still, it was strange. As he took a step to investigate, to push it up and see if it was a hiding spot, the door creaked open.

In walked Rylee, looking like a sweating God.

"Oh." Rylee looked at Drew and froze, as though he was the last person he'd expected to see here.

"Hey." Drew offered a nod and stepped forwards to meet Rylee halfway. "Are you avoiding me?" he asked, deciding to come right out with it. He knew the answer was an honest *yes*, but a dishonest avoidance was more likely. Something to pass off the subject as though it was nothing.

Before Rylee took it there, he stepped close enough to feel the heat from Rylee's body. "It would be a shame if you were," he whispered, reaching with his right hand to hover it right over Rylee's heart. In the split second it took to make the move, Rylee grabbed his wrist and pushed it aside, well away from where it risked making contact.

"Are you afraid to touch me because you're afraid of what I'll do to you?" he asked, smirking as Rylee's eyes became hooded in response to their proximity. He lowered his voice another notch and leaned in until their lips hovered a breath apart. "Or are you afraid of what *you'll* do to *me*?"

The grip on his wrist tightened, but Drew didn't care. He knew Rylee was struggling with his control. He edged closer. Their thighs brushed, while Drew lifted his left hand to cup Rylee's cheek. Rylee released the breath he was holding and his eyelids drooped as Drew dragged his thumb across his pouting lips.

God, he could come from standing here and touching the guy like this. It shouldn't have been possible, but it was intoxicating to see the way he reacted.

Drew let his thumb drag Rylee's bottom lip, then let go and watched it spring back into position. As his hand trailed his neck to Rylee's strong chest, he couldn't help but watch as he parted his lips to swipe his tongue over his bottom lip, exactly where Drew's thumb had been.

"Do I taste good?" he whispered, willing to offer another sample if he asked for it. But he *would* have to ask for it. He was sick of the constant mixed messages.

Yes or no was all he needed.

"Do you realise you sound like a drunken frat boy?" Rylee retaliated, throwing off his touch and taking a step back. He walked around Drew and made his feelings clear by entering the bathroom and slamming the door shut.

Rylee was evil. He let Drew get close, feeling the chemistry between them, then he switched off his emotions as if they didn't exist. But they did and one day he'd have to learn.

A part of Drew understood his reticence. Rylee had been in a long-term relationship with a guy who cheated, lied, and waltzed into the sunset with his damned sister. Drew wasn't that guy. Hell, he didn't sleep around, he didn't sleep with a guy until the third or fourth date and he definitely didn't take relationships lightly. If there came a day when he fell out of love with a partner, he was honest and appreciative enough of their time together to tell them. He would never go out and have an affair, then let them find out in the most heartbreaking way possible.

How could he show Rylee he wasn't that guy if he wasn't allowed to get close? And why did he care?

Okay, he knew why he cared. Rylee was... God, the man was a ridiculous mess of the things he loved, hated, and craved. There was no way he'd be able to resist him for long and he knew it. Drew was trying to accept it. He was trying to figure out a way to have what he wanted and needed with Rylee, while still being true to himself and his mission for Sheffield.

He couldn't have it all, but he was trying his damned hardest to get what he could out of this ridiculous situation.

As he debated what to do, Rylee stormed out of the bathroom and stepped close. Drew's instinct was to flinch and take a quick step away.

Those hard, angry eyes softened and the tension in Rylee's shoulders broke into something more relaxed. "I'm sorry I startled you," he said before his voice eased into a natural, calm tone Drew loved. "I wanted to apologise for snapping. It's not your fault we have an attraction to each another, but I did want to tell you I can't allow it. I'm not ready for a relationship, and I'm not interested in a fling. Whatever it is we could have together is impossible."

"Not impossible," Drew argued, keeping his voice quiet and understanding, not wanting to kick off a fight he couldn't win. "Not advisable, right?" he realised. "I mean, we could make it happen and see where it led, but it wouldn't be a smart idea for the captain of the fraternity to get involved with a brother. And, I'm new. I'm not from Vihaan, and I don't know your ways. It makes it harder to connect. It's not worth the trouble."

It hurt to recite the ways they were a horrible match for each other, but Drew couldn't deny it. It was pointless. He ached to have Rylee as his own while terrified of the same.

What would it do to him to get involved with someone running an illegal animal smuggling ring or an underground BDSM club? He'd compromise whatever investigation Sheffield had going. Beyond that, he'd put his heart at risk for a criminal or a kinky Dom or sub, when he couldn't be whatever Rylee needed as his opposite. Drew wasn't anything beyond vanilla. Maybe a pushy bottom. Missionary, doggy, or even Ride the Cowboy suited him; he didn't need anything more.

It would be nice to get *something,* but he wasn't stupid. He probably wasn't Rylee's type. The guy had to be frustrated from always being the leader and having a guy he was attracted to lying in the bed across the room. Not like it made him a compatible partner, but his first night suggested exactly what Rylee had said...they had off the charts compatibility and chemistry. Their attraction steamed the room every time they were alone together.

The two of them together spelled trouble and eventual heartache. If not for Rylee, then definitely for Drew. He wasn't sure he'd survive it a second time around.

Rylee cleared his throat, reminding Drew of their proximity and what he'd said. He took a step back and offered an uncertain smile. This time, Rylee didn't back away. He stepped forwards, grabbed Drew by the shoulders and tugged them chest to chest.

Drew could have fallen into Rylee's dark eyes and stayed lost for days. They drew closer, his eyelids drooped, as he parted his lips in invitation of the kiss he suspected was about to grace his lips.

Slowly, Rylee leaned down, focusing on bringing their lips into contact, though Drew had to rise on his tiptoes to get them close enough.

"Drew!"

They sprang back from each other, Rylee cursing and walking towards his bed, as he raked a hand through his hair.

Drew sighed and pressed a hand to his erratically beating heart.

"Drew, hurry up! I want a damned muffin already!" Keon's voice floated up the stairs with humour and lightness. The sounds he wanted to hear from his friend, who had suggested he shower before their treat and talk.

Slipping over to his bed, Drew dressed and crossed to the bedroom door. With his hand on the door handle, he hesitated. "I'll be right there!" he called, hoping it was enough to keep Keon at bay for another few minutes. Turning, he watched Rylee disappear into the bathroom again, disappointed.

He wasn't giving up easily. No stolen moment they hadn't been allowed to enjoy would make him back off.

He wanted more of those quick, breathless, heart-pounding moments. And he wanted them with Rylee.

Chapter Eight

Keon was in a good mood when Drew made it downstairs. They sat talking over muffins and coffee, saying nothing in particular for over an hour. When Rylee ventured downstairs, and barely glanced their way as he passed by them and proceeded into the kitchen, the conversation took a personal turn.

"What's up with him?" Keon whispered, leaning in close while eyeing the archway into the dining room.

"Something about responsibility and too much pride," Drew replied, trying not to be bitter. It was hard, with Rylee being obtuse. "He's probably looking for someone more...compliant," he hinted, deciding it was the perfect time and circumstances to dig into whether the house was a secret BDSM club. He had to find out from someone and Keon was his best chance.

Chuckling, Keon gave him a nudge. "Compliant? Is he trying to convince you he's a dominatrix or something?" The hint of teasing in his voice suggested his guess of BDSM was way off.

Sighing, since it meant more work, Drew sank into the sofa and chose another muffin. "I don't know. I feel like we're compatible and he keeps saying we're not. The first night I stayed, he jacked off right across the room from me. I thought he needed relief, but he turned and caught me watching through the mirror," he explained, remembering the night in perfect detail. It had been such a surprise and intense.

"And?" Keon pressed.

"He came...and said goodnight, as if he'd been thinking of me the whole time and wanted me to know," he admitted, still not sure what Rylee had been thinking. "I didn't do anything, other than jacking off along with him. I wanted to think, settle in, and figure stuff out. I never hinted there was a chance we'd get together."

His friend nodded and acknowledged what came next, without needing a prompt or a reminder. "Besides, he ignored you after your first night, didn't he?"

"Yeah." Drew shrugged, not knowing what else to say. "I thought he was giving me space to settle in, but the minute I hint at wanting to get closer, he backtracks. Before I came downstairs, I was getting out of the shower," he continued, giving him a brief rundown of what had happened upstairs.

"Wow. That's cold," Keon said, shaking his head as he reached for the coffee table to grab a fourth muffin. "I've never seen him act like this. Blanking *both* of us on the way past...it makes no sense. I know he likes you. It's obvious every time he looks at you. He can't keep his eyes off you when you're in the same room as each other." He said it as if it was a reason to jump into a relationship with Drew.

Rylee seemed settled in his insistence to keep his distance. What was there for Drew to do? Maybe he should move on from the intense feelings he had for Rylee and have fun?

*

Hours later, Drew sat in his room, resting against the headboard, with his laptop on his knee. Rylee had avoided him this afternoon, though the rest of the boys had indulged in his muffins and praised him for making them. Keon had sat and talked for hours, about everything and nothing, but Rylee still hadn't shown an ounce of interest.

Despite his decision to move on, his heart wasn't in it. He wasn't here to flirt, hookup, or find a boyfriend. He was here to do his job and get an escape plan put into order.

Booting the laptop took a few minutes, and then he was ready to open the hidden folder on his desktop to open the files he'd copied from Rylee's USB disk.

The disappointment of Rylee's dismissal wouldn't go away, as he scoured various suspicious photographs. Twenty of the dungeon-type hidden-room in the basement, each with a wild cat sleeping or sitting in the room, with a chain attached to the neck collar, labelled before, during, and after.

Instead of browsing the contents in the folder itself, Drew opened the first photograph and viewed it full-screen. The first image showed a young man whom he'd never seen sitting on the floor sobbing, his hands clasped within the cuffs attached to the wall. It was a little disturbing, unless the BDSM club—which Keon seemed to know nothing about or was tight-lipped about in front of him—had a retraining program he'd read about in a book once. Drew had read about unruly subs enduring isolation, somewhere. It had been a dark fantasy novel and he wasn't sure it was legal or right for a true BDSM relationship. From what he knew, they focused on consent and care.

Drew shook it off and pressed to the right, to view the next picture—the during. Which was confusing, since it showed a black wolf with a nasty scar down its face, from the side of its eye to its chin. It was snarling in the photo.

The after photo was something even more confusing. The wolf lay on an old battered sofa in the basement, sprawled out without a single chain attached.

What was a wolf doing in the house? Who was the young man chained up? Why were they labelled before, during, and after? What did they represent? Was there weird experimentation transpiring here? Was it a matter of a man and wolf taking part in a fight club, with the after picture depicting the winner of the fight?

It was confusing.

Closing the expanded photo window, Drew turned to the other items he'd copied from the USB drive. What looked to be household accounts, a ledger of comings and goings for the other brothers, as well as a few labelled Journal, with the date.

Hovering his finger over the most recent journal entry, Drew couldn't decide whether to open it. It seemed rude to read Rylee's personal thoughts, but he needed to know if he was barking up the wrong tree or if there was evidence inside. On one hand, he needed to acquit Rylee or convict him, but, on the other, he had to find *something* to give Sheffield when he saw him again.

Biting the bullet, he clicked and the document opened. "Here goes." As the document appeared, he closed his eyes and said a silent prayer for something good to come from his snooping. If he found nothing useful, he would have violated Rylee's trust for no reason.

Finally having the courage to open his eyes, Drew peeked first and looked at the mountain of words on the page. Ten pages, which was a heck of a lot for a journal entry.

He began reading the entry for this morning.

I think I'm going insane. It feels like I'm losing control of myself, my cat, and my entire ability to function like a normal human being.

It started the night Drew arrived. The second I saw him on the doorstep, lost and alone, I felt something shift. It was physical, like someone had pulled a string and moved something inside me. My heart pulsed but didn't beat to its usual rhythm. I noticed my vision changing and was shocked to see a flash of red in Drew's eyes.

In a moment, I knew what he was and we were meant for each other. It scared me. I wasn't ready and I'm still not. I didn't want to accept it, but having him in my bedroom was too much to handle. Getting naked and touching myself was cowardly, but better than crawling in beside a complete stranger.

Not like Drew would have argued. I think he would have enjoyed it, since he came right along with me. I still don't know what he sees in me, but I'm afraid he doesn't. I'm scared what draws him to me is the same instinctual force drawing me in, making his eyes flash and my heart pulse the way it did.

If it's true, we're drawn to each other for this reason and no other, I don't want any part of it. I want a relationship with free will, not blind lust and "fate" leading the way. I gave in to the feeling once and it ended in disaster. I got my heart broken for no reason except my own stupidity. I won't do it again.

It's getting harder to avoid him. Drew keeps looking at me like I'm the tastiest treat he's ever seen. He's beautiful, and there are times when he's so sweet I want to hold him and tell him he's safe now, away from his family.

At times, I see him with Keon and the jealousy is uncontrollable. I'm forced to leave the room or go for a run to work off the feeling. Lorcan has noticed and he keeps trying to push me into telling Drew everything—about my past, about the cats, the house, even about Vihaan. I can't risk it. I keep this entire house safe, to the last person. I can't put this at risk for a random guy I'm drawn to, when I can't even figure out how I feel about him.

Hell, I can't decide how I feel about myself. I don't know if I want a new relationship, if I want to take the risk again, if I can face letting someone into my life. If I can't figure it out, how can I decide whether to tell Drew everything he needs to know to help him understand the difficulty of those decisions?

I can't do it.

Opening up would mean putting us at risk. After the last fiasco of the undercover policeman getting in here and nearly discovering the truth, we can't trust anyone. He made us think he was a friend. For all we know, Drew isn't who he says he is, despite everyone arguing otherwise. No matter how many meetings we have to discuss it, no one can see the danger of accepting him into our lives the way I can.

How can I, in clear conscience, let my feelings guide us towards destruction?

Drew sighed and stopped reading. There was more to read, but he couldn't face it. Closing the document, then the folder, he leaned against the headboard. He couldn't think straight.

He'd never imagined Rylee would be struggling with his decision to keep his distance. He'd seemed adamant. Drew had never questioned his need for distance. But it hurt to have an emotional cliff between them impossible to cross alone. He'd need Rylee waiting on the other side if he was going to take the leap.

Now, he wasn't sure what to do. Should he try to show Rylee he could be the person he needed, that it wasn't fate or anything else leading them together but mutual attraction? Or would Rylee never believe anything but what his instincts had already told him?

Drew dropped his head into his hands and groaned. This couldn't end well.

Chapter Nine

Four Days Later

From the moment he left the house meeting, Rylee made sure to avoid Drew, who made a concerted effort to get close at every opportunity. He tried hard not to look or talk unless necessary. They didn't sit beside each other during meals, nor across from each other and Rylee always stayed up until Drew had fallen asleep.

It was infuriating and complicated, but necessary.

Whatever Drew was up to was suspicious. He flipped between hot and cold, and Rylee was getting whiplash.

Hell, the guy was scorching hot, and he'd been more than happy to knock boots with Drew right from his first night in the house. Once he flipped the nervous, shy switch and became flirtatious, Rylee backed off. He couldn't shake the feeling Drew was playing games.

Playing games with a Vihaan was asking for trouble, and he'd had more than enough trouble to last him a lifetime.

Rylee took another sip from his bottle of beer and watched Drew as his thoughts tumbled. He had proven to be interesting in ways other than those which had first attracted him: rude when woken early, unwilling to open up, with a definite chip on his shoulder about being gay, and a serious issue with his father and authority figures.

For the past few days, Drew kept more than a comfortable distance from the rest of the house by refusing to join nights out and not using names because it meant putting in the effort to learn who they belonged to. A lot counted against Drew, while his handsome face, sharp mind, and well-sculpted body continued to draw Rylee in.

Rylee didn't want to want Drew, but with no one else to catch his attention, Drew took most of his time. He watched from afar and wondered if Drew was wearing a mask with them or finally being himself.

Was it possible he was nothing more than a grumpy, flirtatious student with a chip on his shoulder? Or was he more complicated and trying to protect his heart from yet another disappointment? Or protecting himself from *feeling* like a disappointment again?

His dad had done a number on him.

Already in his third year on campus, Rylee had become bored with campus, but he would never get bored watching these lost, lonely guys wandering towards their fraternity in search of a haven and finding their true self. Guys like Delaware, who had drifted in with the snow a year ago, with a black eye and a bloody nose, having escaped his furious mother. The change in him over the last year had been beautiful to see, but also heartwarming.

He loved nothing more than taking in strays, setting them on their feet and watching them make their own lives.

His own life was more complicated. He lived in this house as the owner and the captain. When the students currently living here had left, he would remain, ready to take in any other lost boys who came his way. Once he left campus, he'd still own this house and offer it as a refuge to those who needed it.

His love life remained a mess. It probably always would be.

He was sick of having flings with people who never tried to get to know him. Another reason he'd turned away from his attraction to Drew, despite his sudden interest. One-night stands, cheaters, players, and arrogant assholes who thought they should be the centre of his world without ever making him theirs. He was done with them. He wanted something new but hadn't met the person who could fill the void. He didn't think one existed outside Vihaan.

For now, Drew stole his attention. Though Rylee never planned to do anything, since Drew was the type of guy he was trying to get away from, there was no harm in looking.

"You okay, bud?" a voice asked from his side.

Rylee dragged his eyes away from Drew, who was dancing with a cute blond from another fraternity out on the front lawn. Someone close by was throwing a party and he'd given his permission for the boys to participate as long as they could control themselves. The fraternity had a reputation to maintain. It didn't mean he had to take part. He stood in the living room, by the window, watching his friends and make-shift family have a good time.

His best friend sidled up beside him with a smile.

"I guess," he answered, since there was nothing wrong. He was figuring out a few things.

"Watching Drew again?" Lorcan chuckled.

"Reminding myself why I will never do anything *more* than watch him," Rylee confessed, to make sure his friend got the point. He had no interest in rehashing how pathetic his love life was because he'd shown interest in one man.

A mysterious smile played on Lorcan's lips as he sneaked a glance in his direction. "Who messed you up, Rylee?" he asked. "The four years I've known you, you do everything in your power to make other people happy, but you never seem happy yourself, unless you're with your cat. Did someone do this to you or is this something always ticking away in the background?"

Sighing, Rylee released the tension in his shoulders and thought about the truth. It was more than someone messing him up. If it had been a person, he could have blamed someone else. No, his problem lay deeper. He *knew* he would never find what he was looking for. He had too high expectations to find it on campus, and when would he ever leave? He was needed here. He had a purpose here.

In his thirty years of life, he'd never once met a guy who fit his needs: smart, sophisticated but not arrogant, spontaneous but reliable, attractive but not vain, selfless but not to the extent they couldn't enjoy a luxury now and then. He needed someone good with animals, considerate of others, who liked to help people and could be selfless. He needed someone...well, someone who didn't exist.

"Not a someone," Rylee admitted, refusing to say more. Lorcan was his best friend and had been since they met in a local bar and hit it off over a few beers. As much as he loved him, he couldn't put his thoughts into appropriate words.

He smiled, deciding to throw it out there. If there was anyone open enough to hear his thoughts it was Lorcan. "It wasn't anyone in particular. I see things differently to other people, I guess. I need someone who can accept me the way I am—all of me—without question, hesitation, and without making me out to be a saint. Someone who sees the good, the bad and the dangerous, but still wants me." Rylee shrugged it off as if it was no big deal because it wasn't. He had accepted his fate a long time ago.

He could tell he'd rendered Lorcan speechless. He returned his attention to the front lawn to see Drew heading inside, still swishing and swaying his hips to the music. When Drew walked in the front door and headed for the stairs, Rylee could hear him humming.

It was nice to see him participating and having a good time. Rylee couldn't help but be grateful he hadn't brought the blond twink along.

Lorcan snatched the bottle of beer from his hand and smirked. "Drew's heading upstairs. Go after him," he suggested, completely ignoring Rylee's glare of disapproval to lean forwards. "How do you know he can't give you what you want if you don't give him the chance?"Damn it, he had a point.

*

"Shit." Rylee stalled at the top of the stairs when he saw Keon. He was at the end of the corridor, sitting on the bay window-seat, smoking out the open window.

One of the youngest of the house, Keon had come onto Rylee on his first night, sneaking into his bedroom and attempting to get into bed with him. Ever since, Keon turned on the charm, still looking to hookup. With short dark hair, lovely green eyes and a pleasant smile, it wasn't Keon he had a problem with. It was his massive Daddy-issue which meant every fling he'd had since joining the house six months ago had been tall, buff, and dominant.

Rylee didn't intend to be the next lover for a guy who had a constant need to be loved and cared for by an older man. He didn't want to play the "daddy" or the authority figure. As much as he wanted the guy to be happy, his tumultuous relationship with his older brothers—a pair of bullying assholes—had twisted his head and he was heading straight for trouble if he wasn't careful.

The worst part—absolutely, positively *worst*—was Keon becoming friends with Drew in the last few days, thanks to them both being casual smokers. More than once, Rylee had watched them disappear into the garden for a smoke, wondering if they put more than cigarettes in their mouths.

Jealousy. Such an evil emotion.

Rylee shook it off and approached with a single step, pausing when Keon turned and grinned.

"Were you staring at my ass?" Keon laughed out the corner of his mouth.

"No." He snapped the word out to remind him they would never be together, no matter what he said or did. At least Keon shrugged it off and turned on the seat to face him while taking another drag. Rylee hovered in front of him. "Why aren't you enjoying the party?"

Keon shrugged again, this time lowering the hand holding his cigarette to his knee and staring at it. "I can't say I've enjoyed a party in a long time. Besides, I'm tired. I was thinking of disappearing for the night," he said, the lost note in his voice filled with truth.

"You've grown close to Drew, haven't you?" Rylee reminded him, wondering if this latest melancholy was the breaking point where he admitted his problems.

"Yeah."

"Didn't you want to go hang out with him? He seems to like dancing. Don't you?" he asked knowing fine well he did. Keon shrugged again, and he knew he wasn't helping. He wasn't making a breakthrough. Keon was struggling with something in unnecessary silence.

Rylee was lost. He didn't know what to do to help him. An uncomfortable silence fell between them. Rylee thought about leaving and retreating to his bedroom, to wallow in self-pity and turn over Keon's issues, searching for a solution. He hesitated when Keon opened his mouth to speak, then froze as a slow smile spread onto his lips.

"Drew."

Reluctantly, Rylee followed his gaze and found Drew leaning against their bedroom door, his hands in his jean pockets. Which was a terrible decision, because it tightened his jeans around the hard flesh inside. And it *was* hard, he could see.

It was the soft, warm look in his eyes which touched the spark of loneliness inside Rylee, making his heart jump with an unfamiliar emotion.

"Rylee was trying to encourage me to join the party," Keon said, as he turned and snubbed out his cigarette into an ashtray. "Fancy going out with me to find my party spirit?"

Drew laughed and crossed to stand in front of Keon. With more tenderness than Rylee cared to see, he brushed Keon's dark hair behind his ear and held his hand to the nape of his neck. "No. Why don't we think about this as phase one? You go out there, you find a hot boy to dance with and you can tell me how it went tomorrow? If you don't feel comfortable, at least you'll have tried?"

Curiosity swirled in his gut at the conversation. It sounded like Drew was counselling Keon into being more sociable or facing his loneliness. He wanted to interrupt and disagree, as a hot boy to dance with was not the solution to his problems.

"And you have to promise you won't have sex," he bargained, drawing an eye roll from Keon.

"Fine." He stood and glanced at Rylee, with a smirk. As he kissed Drew's cheek, he could hear the whispered words, "As long as you promise you will."

Chapter Ten

Keon was a little upstart, but he wasn't wrong.

Drew had been trying to draw Rylee's attention for the last few days and had failed, despite the impressive show on his first night. In amongst the flirting and trying to settle into the house, Keon had been opening up more as they became friends. Drew hadn't risked approaching the exotic animal topic yet. He needed to make sure Keon was invested in their friendship before he could expect information, but it was nice to have a friend in this strange place.

When Rylee cleared his throat, he remembered noticing how he managed to hear a hell of a lot of conversations he shouldn't have been able to. He must have incredible hearing. Drew figured he'd heard Keon's counter-agreement.

He had such soft eyes, smooth, perfect skin and loose-fitting, drab clothes that said he didn't care for fashion or about what people thought of him. Drew was captivated, despite the gruff undertones of a hardass who was obsessed with being in charge.

He could work with that.

Stepping forwards, he pressed a hand to Rylee's denim-shirted chest and met his deep brown gaze. "I was about to go to bed. Want to join me?" he asked, deciding to make it clear what he wanted. Flirting, trying to be charming, trying to be subtle hadn't helped. He spelled it out.

He had to. It had already been far too long since they first locked eyes and he knew Rylee desired him. The last few days had been torture, knowing what Rylee wanted, remembering the first night when he jacked off to thoughts of Drew. To realise Rylee wasn't going to act on those thoughts was infuriating.

Drew *needed* him to.

Until he sensed Rylee's eyes crawling over him six nights ago, the lack of another hand on his dick in the last two years hadn't bothered him. He hadn't cared when no one's lips had been on his in twenty-four months. It hadn't registered spending one hundred and four weeks without intimate contact.

Standing there, watching Rylee watching him, Drew was aware of how long it had been and how desperately he wanted this man, in particular, to break the long, cold run of loneliness.

Drew didn't have time to worry he'd turn away. Rylee swallowed and crushed his mouth to Drew's, sending a wave of shock through his system. The moment his lips parted, Drew pushed forwards and cupped both hands around his neck to keep him close. No way was he letting Rylee escape again.

With a groan, Rylee grabbed his waist and lifted Drew off his feet. It was fair turn around to wrap his legs around Rylee's waist and submit to the kiss completely. Thrown against the hardwood of their bedroom door, Drew grunted as his back made impact. Drew fumbled for the door handle with his left hand. They tumbled inside as the door burst open, Rylee's strong legs getting them inside in one piece, and straight for Rylee's double bed.

Grasping at his hair, Drew licked the delicious tongue tangling with his own and tightened his thighs around

Rylee's waist, as he was dropped onto the mattress. His biting grip on Rylee's short, shaggy hair meant he had no chance to retreat. His entire weight fell onto Drew, drawing a delighted moan from his throat. Embracing the crush of a big, strong man like Rylee on top of him.

Drew lost his sense in the wake of pleasure. He gripped Rylee's hips and drew him close at the same time Rylee cupped his ass and hauled him forwards.

The kiss was hungry right from the start, as if they wanted to devour each other, while their hands and tongues and lips explored what was on offer. It bordered on frantic, but he didn't care. He wanted Rylee like he had never wanted anyone else. Kissing him was the most thrilling, meaningful moment of his life. Like his whole world finally came together. It was breathtaking.

He wasn't sure when or how it happened, but one minute he was holding Rylee's hips down to keep them groin to groin, the next thing he knew his hands slipped up the inside of Rylee's shirt, feeling the hard abs underneath. He moaned into his mouth when Drew's drifting touch brushed the surface of sandy hair on his chest. The guys he'd seen on campus were infatuated with their bodies, and bare chests seemed to be a "thing". It was one craze he wasn't remotely interested in. He had never told anyone, but he had an addiction to men with a decent amount of hair. Not rugs and not in odd or off-putting places, but a wealth of chest hair and, as he found on Rylee, a nice amount leading into the cut of his hips. He couldn't suppress his groan. Rylee was too good to be true.

Drew thrust his tongue into Rylee's mouth with renewed vigour, savouring the sweet but diluted taste of beer on his tongue. He wasn't sure he ever wanted to stop kissing him, and by the feel of it, Rylee agreed.

He was happy to lie there and be kissed into a new century. When Rylee's strong hand moved into the space between them and rubbed his hard cock through his jeans, he about bit the tongue invading his mouth.

"I want to fuck you," Rylee muttered, his mouth drifting across his cheek in soft, brief kisses.

Drew's breathing hitched at the thought. He could imagine how incredible a lover Rylee was after their kissing session. He licked his lips as Rylee hovered over him. Drew nodded. He wanted it too.

Rylee reached across to the bedside table and returned with a bottle of lube. He set it on the pillow, as he sat on his knees and unbuttoned his shirt. Drew barely noticed him removing it, he was too busy touching the soft hair underneath and brushing his thumb over the pert nipples buried in amongst it.

Above him, Rylee shuddered and his head dropped back. "Fuck...feels good," he claimed with a moan of approval. Reaching down, he undid the fastening of his jeans.

Drew watched every move, as they were flipped open, drawn down Rylee's hips and under his knees, over his feet and tossed onto the floor. He watched those sharp abs flex and twist as Rylee rose and stood over him on the bed. Removing his shoes, socks and boxers, he stripped naked.

When he sank to his knees, it took Drew's breath away. His hand immediately went to Rylee's chest, pressing his fingertips into his strong pecs, while he rose to kiss those soft lips.

The hungry way Rylee responded, holding his head still and plundering deep, gave him shivers. Their tongues touched, eliciting a low, deep growl from Rylee which was unexpected but exhilarating.

Rylee grabbed Drew's T-shirt at the collar and tugged hard enough the seam burst, the fabric tearing with an audible rip. Drew couldn't care less. He pulled at the tear, lengthening it as Rylee broke the kiss to lure him in with dark, hungry eyes. They worked in unison to rip the last of it and free him.

"Bloody stubborn bastard," Drew complained, smiling at the way Rylee laughed. It wasn't the gruff, stern sound he was used to from Rylee. This was soft and sweet, an acknowledgement of the urgency.

Who could blame him?

Drew lay back, breathing hard, watching Rylee's dark eyes take in every inch of him, stopping at his jeans. Without having to be asked, he began to remove them, kicking off his shoes and lifting his hips from the bed to push off the stupid denim keeping him from experiencing more of Rylee's touch.

The minute they were both naked, Drew wasted no time dragging Rylee's hips to his and grinding against him. The move made his partner gasp and bite his lip while slipping his hand between them.

Rylee was breathing as hard as Drew was, offering the promised touch which began with a fondle and morphed into a more satisfying stroke. He moaned as Rylee kissed the base of his neck, whilst giving his erection a pleasurable tug.

Drew bucked his hips in delight when those talented lips sought out his nipple. He couldn't wait any longer. He needed it and wanted it, and every fibre of his body demanded it. "Rylee...God, I need it..." he panted, arching as he cupped Rylee's perfect bubble butt in both hands. He squeezed, trying to draw the stubborn man closer.

"Please—" His plea ended in a moan, the moment Rylee plastered their mouths together in a long, spine-tingling kiss.

Laying his arms over those strong shoulders, he let slip another moan of pleasure, loving the dominant way Rylee pinned him in place, devoured his kisses and rubbed his huge cock against his own. It was a dizzying combination.

Breaking the kiss but leaving their lips touching, Rylee ground against his aching cock. "Tell me you bottom, or I swear I'll kill you for getting us this far," he muttered, their lips brushing with the words.

Unable to help but smile, Drew stuck his tongue out and licked the seam of Rylee's lips. "Total bottom. Greedy, greedy bottom," he promised, giving his ass another squeeze.

Rylee grinned, feral and gloating. He would have smacked him for it under any other circumstances. Instead, he let it bolster his relief. Which was fine, since those big hands didn't go back to worshipping his dick. He grabbed Drew's hands from his ass and removed them from his hot skin.

"Stay," he ordered, as he lifted Drew's hands and pinned them by his head, at the side of the pillow. As soon as Rylee let go, he grabbed the corners of the pillow. He was too handsy to manage it by will alone.

Not knowing what he wanted—silence, screaming, compliance, or defiance—Drew waited and watched intently.

Sliding out of view, he shivered at the ghostly breath across his cock head. A second later, a hot tongue lapped at the slit and soft lips encased the head, trapping it in Rylee's mouth. "Fuck, feels good." Drew released the pillow with his right hand, to run his fingers through Rylee's thick hair. The caress ended in a tight grip the minute the teasing bastard scraped his teeth against his skin.

God, this was going to be amazing!

Chapter Eleven

Sucking Drew's thick, short dick was a delight he hadn't expected to enjoy tonight. But he didn't want to take it too far, too soon. Rylee ached to bury deep in Drew, eager to find out if he was as greedy as he claimed.

Climbing over his stunning lover, he embraced the hand brushing through his hair in proof of how desperate Drew was. A light tug, urging him forwards.

Rolling to the side, Rylee held onto Drew, reversing their positions. He grasped Drew's tight rear end with his right hand, while grabbing the lube with his left. He squirted out a generous amount, as Drew repositioned to straddle him, leaning down to latch onto his collarbone.

Rylee hummed in approval, loving the rush of blood to the surface, threatening to leave a mark. Coating his fingers, he reached his left hand around Drew's waist and slid his finger between those pert cheeks to brush the tight hole he found there. God, he was tight and the immediate tensing of puckered skin against his fingertip made him hungry.

Drew moaned above him and pulled back from his chest. He panted heavily, as Rylee slipped his finger inside and worked him loose. As he'd suspected, he clenched against Rylee's finger.

They stared at each other for the longest time—Rylee probing gently to loosen the tension, Drew squirming above him as his body adapted to the one, then two fingers scissoring carefully inside him—each breathless, each unwilling to surrender.

When he removed his fingers and slipped in three, Drew arched like a cat, back dipping delightfully. The way his body undulated in a second counter-arch, Rylee wondered if he was going to ride out his fingers and leave it there, but the hand placed carefully on his abdomen slid lower. Long fingers closed around his length, pumping steadily, until Rylee's head dipped against the pillow. He crooked his finger in retaliation, taking pride in the way Drew shuddered against him.

Rylee wanted more, but he could see how much pleasure Drew got from his fingers. He held his needs at bay, while the hand holding him let go and disappointment set in. He loved having Drew's hand on him. Having him let go was almost enough to quell his need for more.

Until Drew looked him in the eye. There was such need, such lust, love and sin, he wasn't sure he should hold his crystalline blue gaze. Drew moved into a crouch above him, pushing his hand away until Rylee knew he didn't want to ride his fingers anymore.

Drew was as speechless as he was, as he watched, waiting to see what would happen next. A light touch enveloped his cock and with a gentle grip, held him in place as Drew lowered his body over his.

Rylee bit his lip and groaned at the feeling of being inside Drew, having his tight heat surrounding him. It was what he'd wanted since he first set eyes on him. And there he was, every inch of hardness inside the Adonis of a man above him. He gave Drew a moment to adjust, then held his hips to steady him as he began to move, thrusting carefully.

Each rise and fall of the smooth, panting chest above him captivated Rylee. His single goal tonight was to make it difficult for Drew to breathe through the avalanche of an orgasm he planned to give him.

"Rylee," Drew gasped, meeting every thrust, while his hands drifted over his chest and fingers tangled with the hair there.

Holding Drew in place as he thrust, to feel his lover reciprocating with a downward roll of his hips, excited Rylee more than he could put into words. He had never been in sync with anyone, mirroring each movement flawlessly, the way Drew did. It was hard, fast and brutal, how he wanted it and had imagined, since Drew first arrived. He didn't have the patience for slow and steady. He wanted everything Drew had to give and more.

Watching Drew take his hard cock over and over again was sin itself. The look in his eyes, the slackened mouth, the gasps and pants of pleasure, the incoherent words which fell out of his mouth were pure gold. They coiled in his stomach and tightened in evidence of his building pleasure and the orgasm on its way.

Drew came first, without even touching his dick, a tightening on his already sensitive cock sending Rylee into his own spiral of ecstasy.

Long minutes passed as they tried to catch their breath and make sense of the raging desire between them. As he lay there, staring at the beauty above him, he saw a look in Drew's eyes that made him move. He couldn't label it, but he saw a need there identical to his own.

He sat chest to chest with Drew, pulling him into a hot kiss. His lover kissed back, squirming as Rylee's softened cock began to harden again inside him. Drew muttered something against his lips, but he had no idea what it was. He didn't care. What mattered was Drew leaning back to ride his erection again.

Rylee thrust into him urgently, cupping his hips for leverage as Drew wrapped his arms around his neck. He knew it was wild and reckless and stupid since they barely knew each other and they had forgotten to use protection, but he didn't care. It was too good to care.

"Oh, fuck." Rylee gasped in his ear, enjoying the wonderful friction of being inside Drew and having his hard, weeping cock brushing against his chest. His eyes glued to the sweetness of Drew's open mouth as he rode his cock to heaven.

"Rylee, yes...fuck me," he begged, arching as his thrusts became harder and sharper.

He was first to come, spilling his seed into Drew, who closed his eyes and held on as he took another half dozen thrusts to reach his happy ending. Rylee watched his lover as he held onto him, leaning their foreheads together as he rode out the high. He kept trying to open his eyes, but it seemed difficult. They kept fluttering shut again a second later and Rylee knew it wasn't because of the blissful satisfaction they had reached.

His darkest desires and worst fears confirmed.

Gently, he lowered Drew to the bed and pulled out of him. He could tell by his breathing he was close to falling asleep. Rylee let him drift while he nipped into the bathroom to clean up. He gave Drew a cursory cleaning to make sure he didn't become a sticky, sweaty mess. He checked the sheets, to find they were clean. They'd made their mess on each other rather than the bed, which was a small favour.

Rylee climbed into bed, to lay next to Drew, speechless.

Blue eyes flickered behind heavy eyelids, a faint smile reaching his kiss-swollen lips. "Incredible," Drew whispered, reaching out to trail his fingertips over Rylee's chest. Playing with his chest hair, causing multiple nerves to fire.

"Yes, it was," he agreed, loving the husky tone of his sleepy voice.

A frown marred Drew's forehead, and Rylee instinctively reached out to smooth the creases. His actions drew a smile from his lover, as he sighed in contentment and reached to curl his fingers around Rylee's. With the laziness of fatigue, Drew brought his hand to cup his cheek and nuzzled into it.

It was such a...God help him, but *sweet* described it best. Never in his life had he used the word for someone he was attracted to. But it was true. Drew's soft, dreamy gaze, the way he sighed in post-sex bliss were nothing but sweet. Even the way he thought, the things he said, the way he was quiet in bed...it proved his sweet man was an enigma.

Passionate, tender, needy, and with an explosive temper, Rylee had never met anyone he couldn't figure out. Even when people like Delaware and Keon walked through the door, he usually knew their issues within hours, though the solutions to help them often eluded him. It wasn't true with Drew. Rylee couldn't read him.

"What was I—" Drew asked, with a hint of confusion. It took a moment for the look to clear and the smile to return. "Did you clean up?"

"I did," Rylee answered, intrigued to hear he'd put those pieces together, though he looked ready to pass out at any minute.

Humming, he nuzzled Rylee's hand again. "I...passed out? Fell asleep?" he questioned.

Leaning in, Rylee kissed his frown away and lay on his side to watch Drew fight the need to sleep. "You drifted for a while, but you need to sleep," he soothed, reaching to the bottom of the bed to lift the covers he hadn't realised had been kicked to hell with their antics.

The consequence of not making his bed this morning. He'd been in too much of a rush to avoid Drew and look how it had turned out.

With a brief nod, Drew gave a silent agreement but refused to give Rylee his hand back. He liked Drew using it as a pillow, but he couldn't help wondering what the fuck he'd been thinking when he let this happen. He'd been adamant he wouldn't fall for the flirtatious and complicated Drew. He knew what would happen. He always knew, and this time couldn't be any different.

Except...

Well, Drew had a secret, and it wasn't the reason he'd fallen asleep after sex.

Even if he'd been reckless enough to do this on purpose, Rylee had rules. Strict rules demanding his lovers meet certain requirements. They had to pass certain tests, both in personality and prospects. Drew had done none of that. He was still such a mystery; Rylee barely knew him.

Why would he go against his rules after a little over a week with someone he barely knew, when the rules existed for a reason? Why had he given in to their attraction to each another and let them have sex when it went against everything he believed in? He'd been avoiding Drew all this time, to fail at the last hurdle?

He couldn't fathom it. Something was drawing them together. Good or bad didn't matter. Whatever happened now, he would deal with the consequences. But there would be hell to pay if anyone thought he'd give Drew up. He didn't break his rules for any piece of ass that walked into his life.

If Drew was enough of an addiction to get this far, Rylee would kill rather than let him go.

Chapter Twelve

Rylee woke in the morning with a weight on his chest. It wasn't uncomfortable and was warm. His brain fuzzy from sleep, when he looked to see what it was, he was momentarily surprised to see Drew snuggled into him.

Once he'd had time to wake, he couldn't help but enjoy the feeling. It had been a long time since he'd woken happy, with another guy in his bed. But there was a huge problem and he didn't know how long they had before it would *be* a problem. For now, he'd enjoy this moment and hope the bubble didn't burst

Rylee combed his fingers through Drew's hair as he contemplated the possible outcome of the next few days. Drew snuffled into his chest, utterly adorable and he tried hard not to smile but failed.

Drew's hand brushed his chest as he woke, curling around his neck. Slowly, his lover's entire body pushed towards his, but Rylee tried not to react. A knee nudged its way between his thighs and Drew dragged the sole of his foot over the back of Rylee's calf.

It was evident the act was an unconscious search for heat, as Drew was trying to get as close as possible. It didn't stop Rylee's body reacting. He kissed Drew and smiled as the hand on his chest clawed in response. Drew's fingernails were short, leaving no damage beyond a surprisingly pleasant snag against his chest hair. The second time, he was forced to shift into the touch, seeking more.

The moment the brief kiss was over Drew's lips parted with a breath and his eyelids flickered once, twice, and finally opened. They dipped seductively as Rylee offered another kiss. He was delighted when Drew responded with a nip to his bottom lip and trailed his hand up Rylee's chest into his hair. Fingers gripped at the base of his neck, and Drew pulled closer, where Rylee could wrap his arms around him. He wondered if they might descend into round two when a quiet beep suggested an alarm had been set.

"Shit," Drew whispered against his lips.

"Yours?" Rylee realised, surprised since Drew had barely left the house except to walk in the garden and dance on the front lawn for the party last night.

Nodding, his lover stole a last kiss and pulled away to roll onto his back. The fingers in his hair released their grip and ghosted his jawline on their way to the bed. "I forgot. I promised to meet my brother for lunch," Drew explained. He took a moment to scrub his face with both hands, then turned to smile at Rylee. "I'm sorry. I would love to continue this, but if I don't go, he's going to keep crawling up my ass. He'll eventually get what he wants."

The imagery was...interesting.

Rylee couldn't be mad. It was a Saturday morning and there had been nothing to tie them to each other. Besides, Drew wouldn't appreciate Rylee trying to curb his movements or track them after one night of sex. No matter how good it had been.

He had to be careful, here.

"It's okay. I have a book to review," he recalled, letting Drew off the hook. Later tonight, they'd have to talk about what this was and the consequences. Right now, Drew was exhausted and in a hurry.

"Ooh, the new science fiction story?" he asked, turning to slip out of bed. "I want to hear about it when I get back. I love the author and I've been waiting ages for them to release something new." Drew yawned as he stood and wobbled.

Rylee reacted instinctively. He shot across the bed and placed a steadying hand on the small of his back.

"Thank you." Shaking it off, Drew widened his eyes and shook his hands by his side. "I agreed to meet him for lunch, but I never said I'd eat. Fancy going out for brunch first?" he asked, already heading for the bathroom.

A smile tried to twitch onto his lips, but Rylee resisted. Brunch was not a commitment, though Drew putting off his brother to spend time with him certainly sounded like one. Still, no point raising his hopes. "Sure," he called, stretching.

The sound of the shower running negated the possibility of being heard.

Drew reappeared fifteen minutes later, showered and brushing his teeth as he ventured to his dresser to remove a change of clothes.

"I thought you said you were going to meet your brother tomorrow?" Rylee recalled, having had time to think while Drew was in the shower.

For a guy who didn't get along with or like his family, he gave in to their demands. The part of him used to reading people and trying to help them said it was nothing more than Drew trying to salvage whatever essence of family he could. Which was understandable, though it wasn't wise to continually end up surrounded by people who degraded and hurt him.

If they put a proper name to this later, he'd try to make Drew see he was self-sabotaging by being the bigger person and holding hope for something which would never happen.

Drew placed a change of clothes onto his bed, at the side of the room, and disappeared into the bathroom. He spat and water ran, then he reappeared sans toothbrush and shrugged. "Sheffield's "busy" tomorrow. Which, knowing him, is code for a family deal I'm not welcome at," he explained, while pouring his ass into a pair of boxers which fit snugly. "Eyes up top, tiger."

Rylee snapped his gaze to Drew's, to find him grinning and his cheeks flushed. He realised what he'd been caught doing and smiled to show he didn't care.

"Yes, my brother is a bastard, and my family are evil personified," he allowed, gesturing as he dressed and talked at the same time. The tight black jeans he pulled on showed off his ass perfectly, the T-shirt offered a semblance of frat-boy to the outfit with the college logo wearing a beer hat emblazoned on the front. "Right now, my dad is paying my tuition, my brother needs help with a project at work, and I'm playing the good gay son at the work events to make sure I keep them sweet long enough to get me out of this dump." He stopped, halfway through pulling on his T-shirt, to frown. "Well, this place isn't a dump. The town sure is. Or maybe it's my shitty family," he mused.

A part of Rylee wanted to scream *yes* and keep him walking the introspective line, to realise the last part was the real truth he was looking for. Instead, Drew tugged the shirt into place and crossed to where he still lay in bed. His lover climbed on to sit on his knees and ducked to kiss him.

"Are you getting out of bed so we can get brunch?" he asked, a cheeky, teasing lilt to his voice Rylee had never heard. He loved it.

"I'll wait here while you head out and get it for us, then we can eat in bed," he admitted, relishing the thought of lazing in bed and waiting for Drew to return.

Humming, Drew showed enough sign of intrigue to convince him he'd get his way. "Fine. I'll grab us brunch, but when I get back, you better not have any clothes on," he warned, turning to slide off the bed again. Once he was on his feet, he took one last look at Rylee and sighed as he left the room. It had to be a good sign.

*

Twenty minutes later, Rylee was about to give in and catch a few more minutes of sleep when Drew returned.

"I had to wait in a ridiculous queue for this. You better like it," he said, climbing onto the bed while handing over a brown paper bag.

The grease gathering at the bottom didn't look promising, but Rylee kept quiet as he popped the bag open. Inside, to his astonishment was a *Red Blooded Male* burger from the food truck which didn't often make it to campus. He swallowed and glanced at Drew as he delved into what was known as a *Virgin Sauce Tortilla Wrap*.

"Is it okay?" Drew asked, while wiping a bit of hot sauce from the corner of his lips. He looked worried, and Rylee couldn't explain why there was no need.

"It's perfect," he promised, adding a smile for reassurance. Drew returned it while taking another bite and Rylee couldn't help but ask, "What made you choose this truck? I mean, it's my favourite place to eat, but not many people know about it." How the hell had Drew found it?

His lover shrugged and chewed. "Honestly, I've never seen it advertised, but it was on the corner and fifteen people queued outside. I figured it must be good. It would have taken as long to go into the village and find somewhere reasonable as it would to wait in line. I waited," he explained, still with an easy smile that said everything was fine.

Except, it wasn't. Not by far. But he couldn't tell Drew.

Rylee nodded and tucked into the food, moaning in approval for the unique taste assaulting his senses. "So good," he muttered, his mouth unapologetically full. He didn't often delve into a *Red Blooded Male* burger, with too many good choices on the menu, but there was nothing better after a night of hot sex with one of the sexiest little kittens he'd ever met.

Drew giggled and held his hand over his mouth as he finished chewing.

"What?"

"Sorry, I know you didn't speak but," he stopped to lick sauce from his bottom lip and chuckled again, "I remembered something. It must have been from last night? From when I was tired and didn't remember you cleaning up? You called me *'the sexiest little kitten'*," he explained, smiling wide and free, as though he loved the nickname.

Rylee found it infectious. Soon they were both grinning like fools and trying not to laugh as they ate together. They talked about ways to spend their Sunday together, a surprising request Drew beat him to, and silly gossip they'd heard about their housemates and classes.

It was the nicest brunch he'd ever had.

Chapter Thirteen

Leaving Rylee was hard when Drew knew what he was about to do. There was nothing for it, he had to go, or Sheffield would send the troops in thinking he'd been kidnapped or held hostage.

The problem was he hadn't discovered anything. He'd tried, but there was no sign of animals on the property, nothing but hints and insinuations from the boys, and a lot of talk about cats and in-house jokes which didn't make any sense.

When Drew walked into the restaurant where he'd agreed to meet Sheffield—his idea, because his idiot brother wanted him to visit the police station, which would have given him away if anyone dared follow—he removed his jacket and bypassed the maître d'. Sheffield hovered by a table, talking on his mobile while pacing.

It didn't look good.

As soon as he spotted Drew approaching the table, he said a hurried goodbye and snapped the flip phone shut. A flip phone. Drew shook his head but refused to argue about it again. How Sheffield managed to be one of the top detectives in his precinct while being technologically incompetent enough to still own a four-year-old flip phone was beyond him.

"Hey, you're on time," Sheffield noticed.

Trying not to roll his eyes, Drew took a seat and poured a glass of water from the jug on the table. He was pleased to see Sheffield had a coffee and two glasses sat on the table for the water, saving time. The less time he had to spend here the better. He waited for Sheffield to sit. "I'm not eating, and I can't stay long. I have a class to get back for," he said, dropping his first lie of many.

Sheffield raised an eyebrow but didn't seem impressed. "You're going to classes?"

"I have to make it look like I actually need to be on campus." Which, at least, wasn't a lie. Drew had attended two classes, both with Keon. He'd gone to reaffirm their friendship and earn his trust, to find out about the supposed smuggling ring. The problem was he was beginning to like the guy—*all* the guys—and he could see Keon being a great best friend.

Sheffield ignored the argument in favour of delving right into the conversation. "Well, if you don't have long, I'll eat after you leave and save the time," he began, dismissing the entire notion of their lunch meeting being at least a little bit about them being brothers. "Do you have anything for me? Any evidence of what they're doing?" he wondered, folding his hands on the table.

"Nothing yet," Drew admitted. He didn't have any proof of anything underhanded happening. "I'm making progress though. I've spent time with the boys of the house, getting to know them and exploring the property. There's a heck of a lot of animal print, animal jokes and talk of cats, but there's no real proof," he explained, lifting his glass to take another sip.

He was definitely not saying anything about Rylee or their night together. It was none of Sheffield's business what he did in his personal life. Drew had no idea why he'd practically passed out straight after their second round, but it wasn't like him. Sure, he knew sex wasn't normally a speech-stealing, heart-pounding, nerve-rattling event. It didn't mean he had a right to get his kicks and sleep either.

He ran his hand over his face, thinking. Yes. It was okay, Rylee had come first, meaning he didn't have the embarrassing situation of getting off and falling asleep before his lover was done.

He didn't want Rylee to be his lover. He wanted a boyfriend, as impossible as it seemed. He hadn't wanted one for such a long time, but no one had ever *been* Rylee and he was beginning to realise how nice it had been to play out their morning together. Waking together, kissing, snuggling, and eating while talking to each other in such a comfortable way.

Drew hadn't had that in such a long time.

Whether Rylee knew it or not, he did *not* fuck and run. He was going to have to find a way of keeping Rylee interested after he'd told the truth about why he was at the fraternity. While trying to find a way of fulfilling his commitment to Sheffield without losing this new life he'd fallen into and loved.

Damn, Rylee was impossible to resist. He was the most incredible man Drew had ever met. He hadn't lied. Rylee was selfless and special, and Drew hadn't felt this way about someone in forever. Despite his best efforts, he always seemed to get used by people. He was also a moron for letting them get away with it. It was damned nice to have someone big and strong like Rylee take care of him instead of using him. He wasn't ready to lose that yet.

"You have nothing?" Sheffield scoffed and shook his head.

"Look, I've been there longer than any of your other spies," he reminded him. "I'm gaining their trust first, before I go delving into topics they know don't concern me. At the moment, all I have are completely harmless inside jokes about cats. Give me a little more time," he insisted, arguing his case the best he could without having prepared for it.

Drew knew he'd been stupid not to have an idea of what he'd say, but he hadn't expected things with Rylee to become complicated. The whole "mission" had become complicated. He didn't want any part in ruining the family bond the fraternity house had created amongst a bunch of misfit boys who needed a home.

Sheffield held his hands over his face, then pushed them into his hair. "Okay. I can buy you another fortnight, but you better have something useful for me," he agreed, pretty harried for a guy who was in charge of this investigation. "The boss is on at me every minute about what you've found and why it's taking this long."

"Sheffield, these are college guys," Drew reminded him. "They go to classes, have a social life and, if they're criminals, they also have a secret business to run. The amount of time they spend in the house is limited, leaving me limited opportunities to get them alone and vulnerable or trusting enough to tell me the truth. Give it time," he asked, trying to remind Sheffield to be reasonable.

His "mission" wasn't the sole concern in his life.

*

Conflict of interest was one way to put it. Seriously fucked was another.

Drew trudged to campus, enjoying the summer sun and lamenting over how shitty his meeting with Sheffield had been. A fortnight. Then Sheffield's boss pulled the plug on his undercover work and dragged his ass off campus, revealing his dirty secret.

Stopping at traffic lights, he pressed the cross button and waited. Sweat was beading on his neck, trickling down his spine and forehead, but every time he wiped his face he sensed it building again. He couldn't figure out what was happening, since the sun was out but there was a chill wind which wasn't unusual for their little village.

When the coast was clear, he crossed the road and contemplated what he was going to do next. It seemed logical to tell Rylee the truth or end whatever last night had been, and he wasn't the kind of guy who fucked and ran away. It was the reason he'd fallen into endless crappy relationships over the years. He had to face facts, he was drawn to losers. Rylee was the first time he'd ever attracted the attention of a decent guy. He didn't want to screw it up.

Rubbing his forehead as fatigue hit him hard, Drew kept walking to campus and plotting the best way to leave this mess of a mission intact. He had to tell Rylee the truth about the investigation, saving Lorcan, Delaware, Keon and especially Rylee from the possibility of arrest or worst. If they ran an illegal trading business, they had to fix the mess themselves, shut down, and destroy the evidence.

Drew would give them a chance to confess and save themselves. It would ruin Sheffield's investigation, but he had never been much of a brother and it wasn't like his career would suffer for not completing this one investigation. There would be others to help him climb the ladder.

As he entered the fraternity house and headed upstairs to what was becoming *their* room, Drew knew he couldn't turn in the people who lived here. He'd finally found a home—somewhere he belonged—and he wouldn't let Sheffield take it from him.

"Hey, Drew."

He nodded to a guy whose name he still couldn't remember, passing him on his way into his bedroom. He found it empty, which wasn't much of a surprise, since he hadn't expected to find Rylee still lazing in bed. He'd been gone a good hour because of the travelling time there and back again.

Drew could hear humming in the shower, as he dropped his jacket on his bed and proceeded into the bathroom. After shutting the door, he stripped off his clothes, despite the chill to the room. He headed for the shower, biting his lip, to find the glass was steamed, a shadow moving around behind. He headed straight over, opened the door and stepped into the scorching cascade of water.

Rylee pushed his wet hair out of his face and Drew could tell from the languid movements he wasn't long awake or at least still exhausted. Drew stepped in behind him, not too close, and slid his hands over those flat hips, letting them follow the vee cut in his body to the partially hard cock.

"Thinking about me?" Drew teased.

"God, you know how to touch a guy," Rylee breathed out.

Drew took a half step to bring their bodies flush. He started slow, with no idea why he was hooked on the man in his arms. Every breath was captivating. No matter what he said or did, he always wanted more. It seemed Rylee agreed.

He brushed ghostly fingertips over the length of his hardening cock and watched the reaction it bred. Rylee shivered against him. The moment he added the touch of his lips to his neck, Rylee pushed his tight ass against his own hard cock. "Fuck," he approved, making Drew smile. He pushed back to let him know he agreed.

"You have to know someone to be able to touch them right," he whispered in his ear.

"As hot and incredible as you are," Rylee replied softly, "we barely know each other. But, every time you touch me it feels like you know me inside out."

Drew laughed, appreciating the compliment. "Yeah." He nuzzled his earlobe and nipped it playfully. "I feel like I know you real well," he admitted, kissing his way along Rylee's jawline until he could kiss his lips. His shower-mate reacted instantly, both hands going to the crown of his head to encourage him.

Drew didn't need it but accepted it, even as he removed his fingers and moved around to stand in front of Rylee. He didn't look disappointed to find the touch gone.

"We broke my rules this morning," Rylee mentioned, against his lips. "I don't fuck around without going on a first date, and I don't screw around without expectation of a relationship."

Drew had never imagined Rylee would feel the same way, but he didn't argue. Drew had always known there was more to Rylee than the gruff, sexy man who teased and tried to ignore him. Seeing this gentler side, the side that wanted a relationship and wanted to make those needs clear before they went further was a welcome revelation.

"Well" –Drew caught Rylee's eye and smiled– "if you think about my first night here as our first date, last night would have been our fourth or fifth. Technically, we didn't break your rule," he reasoned, watching those kissable lips twitch into a faint smile. "We've been circling each other for days, and neither you nor I fuck around indiscriminately. You could say we've been dating since we met. Unofficially," he concluded.

A rumble of laughter escaped Rylee as he nuzzled against Drew's forehead, to his cheek and placed a chaste kiss on his lips. "I like the sound of that. Are we a couple, now?"

Drew lifted his arms over Rylee's shoulders as he thought it over. "I'd definitely call you my boyfriend," he admitted, tracing his fingers in invisible patterns over the back of Rylee's neck. Unable to resist, he leaned in, kissed Rylee and hoped he wasn't overreacting by believing his instincts which told him Rylee was *the one*. He'd never experienced the feeling, but wanted to hold it close and protect it. At least until Rylee knew the whole truth.

When his lover brushed a hand through his hair, Drew cursed himself for acting catlike, by butting into his hand in approval. It was too good to resist, even if Rylee did laugh.

He kissed him, because he wanted to, and was happy when he was kissed back sensually. There was no rush, no surge of passion or desperation. It was a moment of pure appreciation, where they kissed for the simple pleasure of kissing. He felt wanted and loved like no one else had ever made him feel. He barely knew what to do.

Those soft lips opened for him and their tongues touched. Drew moaned and tilted his head to deepen the kiss. It lasted until Rylee backed away and kissed Drew's jawline.

Drew sank into his arms on instinct, holding Rylee and wanting to be held for a moment. It was irrational, but he knew it was what he wanted. He'd felt off-kilter today and it helped to be in Rylee's arms and know there were no expectations, no rush, and no need to be anyone but himself.

It eased the exhaustion weighing on him.

Rylee responded by wrapping strong arms around him and brushing fingers through his hair, which was more soothing than Drew was willing to admit. He shut the water off, after a few luxurious minutes, and stepped away.

Drew was too tired to move but managed a smile when his newly minted boyfriend returned with a towel and began drying him off lazily. He tried to help but was brushed off.

"You feeling okay?" Rylee asked with worried eyes, guiding him out of the bathroom and back to the bedroom.

Drew managed a nod while crawling onto the big, comfy double bed. "Tired," he confessed. He had never been this tired, but he couldn't lie. He wanted to sleep. "I'm such a liar," he whispered, feeling the weight of those words settling heavily on his shoulders.

"What have you lied about?"

"I feel like I'm living a lie," he confessed, though he'd had no intention of saying it out loud. "I'm lying to you, to the boys in the house, to my brother and my family. I'm beginning to question who I am...which life is the real one and which me is the real me." It was...exhausting.

Rylee sighed heavily as he joined him in bed. "I see. Want to tell me what you're lying about?" he asked, his voice soft and understanding, despite what he'd said.

"Nope." Drew nudged in to snuggle against Rylee's chest, where it was warm and comfortable. "I need to think. I can't tell you if it'll make you go away." Losing Rylee would make the last few days completely pointless. He'd leave his new boyfriend feeling like he couldn't be trusted.

How could he do that?

Rylee wrapped comforting arms around him and held him close. "I hope you'll tell me when you're ready. And I trust you wouldn't be here with me unless you wanted to be," he whispered, his embrace warm and welcome.

Drew couldn't find the energy to reply. He brushed his cheek over Rylee's chest and let the sweet sleep of Morpheus take him.

Chapter Fourteen

Rylee was concerned the next morning when Drew proved impossible to wake. He left him in bed, hoping a few more hours of sleep would rouse him for something to eat. Once he showered, dressed and appeared in the kitchen, it proved more difficult than getting through the day and waiting for Drew to wake.

"Where's Drew?" Keon asked, cornering him in the kitchen the moment he was spotted. "He said we'd talk over breakfast. I thought you'd be down together since…well, you know," he added, with a smile and a wink.

Which eliminated any hope of keeping their night together to themselves. Clearly they'd been discovered and their previous day alone together in his bed hadn't gone unnoticed. "He's sleeping. He went out yesterday to meet his brother for lunch, but came straight back and flaked out. I haven't been able to wake him since," he explained, knowing it wasn't normal.

By his calculation, Drew had been asleep for approximately twenty-one hours, almost an entire day. If he didn't wake soon, Rylee would have to resort to extraordinary measures to make sure he had something to drink or eat.

Keon looked concerned and nibbled his bottom lip. "Is he sick?"

"No. Tired," Rylee replied, still not sure what was happening, though he had a vague idea. There was no point explaining it to Keon, since he had no proof he was on the right track. Leaving the poor guy to wait for Drew to wake, he ventured into the dining room, tapped Lorcan's shoulder and nodded him out of the room in a request for privacy. It was time to discuss what he'd been too afraid to think too deeply about, to find out if he was alone in seeing the signs.

As soon as he and Lorcan ventured to the garden and perched on the bench, Lorcan spoke. "It's happening, isn't it?"

"Yes." He breathed a sigh of relief, knowing he wouldn't have to say the words. "I can't think of any other explanation for why he's sleeping this much. He feels at home here. With us."

"With you," Lorcan agreed, pointing out a truth he hadn't wanted to think too hard on. "I won't pretend to understand why you keep putting distance between you, but I hope you won't do it from now on. He isn't strong enough to handle it. Not after you started this in the first place," he reasoned.

Logically, Rylee knew he was right. This was his fault. He'd started it on the night they met, when he first locked eyes with Drew. Not like Drew had any idea what was happening, but it had been getting worse since then.

Lorcan sighed and grabbed his hand. "Rylee, you've already completed three stages. You have to make sure to follow through with the fourth before Drew suffers any more. And you have to find out if stage five is needed," he continued, too damned reasonable to be angry.

He nodded. "I'll try," he promised, knowing stage four would have to be completed today. Five stages had to be completed by the turn of the new moon in two nights time. If Drew had waited for the new moon to disrupt his life, they'd have more time.

"There's no trying here, Rylee," Lorcan objected quietly and calmly. "You have to go upstairs, complete stage four and check to see if stage five is needed. You can't leave it too long. If it's not needed, then it's a matter of time. Nature will take its course, eventually."

Nodding, he was left with no choice. Lorcan was right, as always. If he didn't complete stage four and stage five wasn't necessary, he'd be leaving Drew is a horrendous state of living a half-life and being mentally incapable of surviving it. The best-case scenario was mild insanity, the worst was full-blown whack-a-doo, loop-de-loop; a strait-jacket snarling monster with an appetite for causing pain. He couldn't let that happen. Not to Drew. He was too sweet to live a half-life.

Heaving a sigh, Rylee did as he was told. He rose from the bench and walked into the house with a heavy heart, hoping for the best. Keon stopped him as he reached the dining room and pushed both hands into his chest with such force he stumbled against the wall.

"What the fuck is wrong with you?" Keon shouted.

Since those were the words he was about to utter, Rylee changed tactics. "What are you talking about?"

"You did this to Drew? On purpose?" Keon challenged, eyes already welled with tears. Anyone would have thought this had been done to *his* boyfriend. "Drew is my best friend! He's the nicest person I've ever met and you did this? Against his will?" he continued, drawing the attention of the rest of the house.

Rubbing the bridge of his nose, Rylee gestured towards the meeting room behind him. "Everyone get inside and have the last person shut the door. It's time we talked about this openly, as a house," he admitted, turning side-on to Keon to let him go first. Which he did, flopping into a seat and folding his arms with murder in his eyes.

The rest of the housemates followed, in attendance as it was early in the morning. Once seated and Lorcan walked in to join them, Rylee followed and shut the door behind him.

"First off"—he said, making his way to the chair which always occupied the centre of the circle, for whoever wanted to speak to the group—"anything Drew and I have shared or done together has been done with his full consent and knowledge. He's not a child. He knew what he was getting into." Rylee wanted to make it clear, beyond anything else, for the likes of Keon who thought he'd thrown this at Drew without explaining what it meant.

"The fact he's not handling it well is on him. We're from Vihaan. We know you need to be prepared for this. Since I'm sure you've been spying on us since Drew arrived, you'll know I attempted to keep my distance, and Drew refused to allow it," he explained, hoping to remind them of that important fact to negate any further accusations. "He's been clear about wanting a relationship. Now I've overcome my hang-ups I'm ready to meet him halfway."

Lorcan gave an approving nod and glanced at Keon, who still looked furious.

"I've agreed with Lorcan. Things are moving fast," Rylee continued, shaking his head as he thought about how much time he wished they'd had to do this right. "Drew and I have completed three stages. Once I leave this meeting, I will complete stage four and five, if it proves necessary. I ask you give Drew time and space to adjust. If he's struggling with his decision or regretting it, we'll deal with it when the time comes. For now, I ask for your understanding and help."

A few heads nodded, but most of the house looked unhappy. Keon stood. "Tell Drew I met a cute guy and we didn't have sex. Unlike you, he cares about me, and he's been helping me. He'll want to know." He stormed out and slammed the door behind him.

Rylee turned to Lorcan for an explanation, not understanding the accusation. Lorcan shook his head and dispatched the group.

Something else was happening here he didn't understand, and it was infuriating.

Regardless, Rylee now had a job to do. He left the impromptu meeting and retreated upstairs to his bedroom, where he found Drew exactly where he'd left him. Sprawled across his bed, gloriously naked. His tousled hair gave him an air of innocence, reminding Rylee of the sad, defensive man he'd unearthed beneath the sarcastic exterior. The Drew he could fall in love with. If such things were in the cards for them.

Taking a deep breath, he perched on the edge of the bed and lamented having to do this while Drew was practically unconscious with sleep. But he didn't have much choice. He couldn't wait.

Rylee retreated into the bathroom for a long shower, knowing he was a coward for doing it and putting off the inevitable, but it was necessary if he was going to complete stage four. After towelling off, he didn't bother dressing again. He walked over to his bed, climbed on to straddle Drew and attempted once more to rouse him from sleep.

"Drew," he whispered, patting his cheek lightly to encourage him to open his eyes. "Drew, you have to wake up for me. Please," he begged, not wanting to do this to an unconscious man.

For a second, those eyelashes flickered in an attempt to open. Rylee tried to encourage something more. "Come on, Drew. I need you. Have you ever topped? Because I need you to," he confessed, hitting his right cheek harder as he fought to wake him from such a bone-deep, unnatural sleep.

A soft moan and a wrinkled brow were his answer.

"Come on!" Rylee practically shouted, as he slapped his cheeks harder. "Drew, I need you to wake up. Open your eyes, give me a nod or a sign you're okay with this. Please," he begged, knowing it was probably pointless but refusing to stop. Pointless didn't equal impossible. Just improbable. "Damn it. Drew, you have to wake the fuck up!"

Drew sighed and his eyes finally opened. He hummed questioningly, to which Rylee laughed. Then he got his wits together.

"Baby, you've got to tell me it's okay for me to ride you. I need it," he whispered, hoping to encourage him to wake, to hear him properly. There was no reaction initially when Rylee pulled back the covers and exposed Drew's nakedness to the cold air of the room.

Finally, his lover moaned in complaint and reached blindly for...something. Rylee had no idea if it was for the covers or for him. "I want you to fuck me," he repeated, trailing his fingers down Drew's exposed chest.

"Yeah." Drew's lips twitched and he moaned, arching into the touch. He muttered something mostly unintelligible, but Rylee was sure he heard "hurry up" in there somewhere. Then it happened. Drew opened his eyes, gaze wild and blown in proof his worst fears had become a reality. "Rylee..." He had no time to react to the plaintive whine. Drew lifted off the mattress and pressed a kiss to his lips.

Finally! It was necessary to complete the stages, but he needed Drew to be in this, to be aware and give his consent. He couldn't have done it otherwise.

It was a relief to hear Drew's soft moan, the feel of his hand brushing his chest. Proof he was more aware. Rylee basked in the reaction, the deep kiss and dragging tongue sweeping across his own. He sighed when Drew dragged his mouth along his jaw and down his neck, leaving breathy kisses across bare skin.

Opening his mouth to make one last request for agreement, he paused at the sound of the door creaking open. There in the doorway stood Keon. Jaw clenched, flask in one hand, and determination in his eyes.

"I need him to be okay," he said, crossing to the bed, where he gave Rylee a shove until he willingly moved aside. Staring in pleasant surprise as Keon fussed over Drew. Petting his hair, murmuring reassurance, promising to take care of him, while encouraging him to sit up and sip from the flask of coffee.

Rylee watched in amazement as Keon did what he hadn't thought to. He hadn't expected it to work, but Drew began to improve, little by little. Enough to frown at Keon, turn curious eyes Rylee's way and accept his smile of reassurance as enough not to fight the process. He cooperated long enough to drink a third of the flask with Keon's help, then curled his hand around it.

With a sign of conscious movement, Keon glanced at Rylee. "Take care of him," he said, placing a feathered kiss to Drew's brow before taking his leave.

Lowering the flask, Drew eyed him carefully. "Want to explain?"

The sound of his voice, natural and strong, made Rylee smile. He placed a kiss to his not-so-fevered brow and heaved a sigh of relief. "Later," he promised, offering encouragement to keep drinking.

By the time the flask was done, Rylee helped him into the shower and spent a pleasant few minutes washing him, while Drew rested against him. Trusting his strength and basking in the attention.

He switched the water off and brushed his hand through Drew's hair, happy to see his lover turn and offer a smile. It lasted until those soft lips pressed to his, light fingers dancing over his hip even as Drew pressed him against the wall. Considering Rylee's plans, and needs, he had no objection. It was much more pleasant to let Drew seduce him than to worry he was taking advantage of a man who may not be in his right mind, or fully conscious.

He wasn't sure he could have lived with himself if it had come to that.

The next few minutes were a blur of heat and passion, with Drew practically rubbing against him. It took Rylee's full strength to lift him off his feet, carry him back to bed, and get a last vocalisation for his own peace of mind. "I need you, baby."

Drew smiled and bit his bottom lip, as though shy and delighted by his slip of the tongue. "I don't...I mean, I haven't for," he stopped with an embarrassed laugh and caught Rylee's face in both hands to draw him in for a kiss. "Yes. Please," he clarified.

There...the look in his eyes...was what he needed. What he had been waiting for.

Trusting they were in this together, he grasped Drew's dick in one hand, and bent to lavish it with attention. It took a few minutes of sucking and licking before it grew to full hardness in his hand, delicious sounds streaming from Drew's lips. As he didn't have the patience for foreplay or dragging it out, Rylee straddled his lover and eased Drew's thick cock into his tight hole.

Drew groaned, low and deep, with a rumble so familiar it made his heart sink. His hands drifted everywhere, roaming with desperation. His eyes bright and wide, alert when he met Rylee's gaze with a feral grin. Refreshed by a copious amount of coffee and a hot shower, returning him to the eager, but fully conscious man he needed right now.

Drew mashed their lips in a kiss all need and teeth and grabbed his cock to stroke him slowly. Teasing.

He'd done this once, with his ex, in the way of Vihaan tradition. It had been so long he had to grit his teeth against the rush of conflicted pain/pleasure receptors which fired on the first push. Despite the time he'd spent in the shower, his hole didn't want to be stretched or to accept Drew as stage four demanded. But he didn't have a choice, and they were running out of time.

He pushed back slowly, taking every inch of Drew's glorious cock inside him. Having gone to the brink in the shower, Rylee needed a few stuttered thrusts against Drew's dick. Below him, Drew's eyes flickered and his lover moaned. His body moved with languid sensuality, back arching, hips thrusting, hands grasping. Every part of him trying to participate despite the hormones flooding him, insisting he rest.

Those eyes and the intensity of every emotion he saw flickering behind them helped Rylee succumb to his orgasm. Those eyes and grasping hands told him he wasn't in this alone. Drew stopped to watch him ride the high, then chased his own. His muscles instinctively clenched around Drew's dick, intensifying each thrust until Drew burst inside him.

"Oh God!" Rylee tipped his head and sighed as a rush of adrenaline shot through him. It was like every nerve in his body sparked like the Fourth of July and breathing was no longer a concept he understood.

His entire body shook as he climbed off Drew and lay beside him. As he feared, not even the coffee could combat what was happening inside Drew, and he had to watch his lover curl onto his side with a sleepy smile. Eyes closing, barely registering his presence, as he once again fell into peaceful, oblivious sleep. Now stage four was over, Rylee had to fight the urge to join him. There was one more stage left.

It took a few minutes for his muscles to agree to move, helping him onto his knees beside Drew. With clinical awareness, Rylee inspected every inch of Drew he could, carefully turning him onto his front to check his back. Which was when he found them. Four scratch marks on the back of his left hip, with three more on his upper right shoulder.

His heart sank to realise he had been too busy avoiding Drew he never saw them before. Never noticed. If he'd kept his damned eyes open, he could have avoided this.

Tracing his fingertips over the shoulder marks, Rylee closed his eyes to find an image in his head of Drew in bed with another man. Of Drew later being dragged out of the bed, tossed onto the floor and towered over by a man with anger in his eyes. A man who didn't like Drew landing safely and grabbed him by the waist with one hand. Digging his nails in and scraping them over his flesh.

Drew cried out in pain and it broke Rylee's heart.

The man grabbed Drew by the hair, dragged him onto his knees and forced his cock into Drew's mouth, gagging him. Unrelenting, he dug his nails into Drew's shoulder to hold him in place, whispering promises of more pain if he didn't *be a good boy* and do as he was told.

Rylee flinched away from such an awful scene. The terrified look in Drew's wet eyes as he tried not to cry had been too much for him to look any further. He knew how the marks had found their way onto his body and he knew why. Punishment. Torment. Torture. Along with a heavy dose of vindictiveness.

He hadn't only seen the event through the bastard's eyes, he'd felt his surety this would be the last time he *allowed* Drew any part of him. He was going to throw him away, to eliminate Drew from his life. Discard him. First, he left the parting gift of new physical, mental, and emotional scars to take with him. Rylee didn't doubt they were a precaution in case the sadistic bastard changed his mind and wanted to drag Drew into his bed again. An insurance policy to instil compliance. A warning of what happened when Drew dared say no.

He couldn't imagine how relieved Drew must have been when the relationship ended. Or was he devastated, because he'd suffered for something fleeting? Perhaps he missed the violent bastard because he'd been brainwashed into loving him and his rough treatment, regardless of how worthless it had made him feel?

Rylee wouldn't know without asking Drew, but it would be too much to ask now, with everything else happening.

He had the answers he needed to move forward. Stages one to four were complete and, God help him, stage five was now not necessary, and a problem.

Because Drew had no idea what had been done. Or what he'd participated in with Rylee. How was he going to tell him?

Chapter Fifteen

Two Days Later

It was time to tell the truth. Rylee knew but he couldn't do it. Not when Drew was having such a hard time adjusting. Yet, it was the reason to tell him everything.

There was no guarantee how he'd take it.

The problem wasn't in how to tell Drew something he'd never believe, it was in the mistake he'd made believing Drew had entered into their mutual attraction and relationship fully aware of the truth. Rylee had thought they were the same and the stumbling block would be trying to explain Vihaan to someone who wasn't native to the land, believing Drew had been raised by Vihaan expats who hadn't taught him how things worked there.

Now that wasn't the case, Rylee was at a loss.

He'd left Drew in his bed, which they'd shared every night since the party, gone for a run, had a shower, and made breakfast. He managed two hours of reading, before he realised it was noon and Drew still wasn't awake. It wasn't unusual, since Drew had spent the last two days going to bed early and waking nearer noon with no concept of why he was tired.

Checking on him one last time before starting his day, Rylee was quiet as he entered the room to find Drew curled up in bed, shivering. He sighed, grabbed the duvet and the blanket from his empty bed and threw it across Drew, where he was already snuggled beneath a duvet of thicker quality than Rylee had bought for the spare bed.

"Rest, sweet cheeks. You're going to need your strength," he whispered, bending to place a kiss on his forehead.

Rylee left him to sleep and returned to the kitchen to wash his lunch dishes. He'd been willing to cook something for Drew if he was hungry, but it was best to let him sleep if he needed to.

"Hey, is Drew coming down?" Lorcan asked, as he joined Rylee in the kitchen.

"No, he's still sleeping." It took a lot to admit, since he knew exactly what conclusions Lorcan would jump to. But he was sick of hiding. Rylee took a deep breath and headed him off. "I need to tell him, but I don't know how to say it and have him believe me. I mean, it's pretty out there and there's no reason to believe it without proof. But proof could send him running," he confessed, needing guidance.

Normally, Rylee was the one telling the boys to trust their instincts, to trust any partner or friend they brought into the secret, but he was the one shielding the others from the rest of campus and the authorities. If he trusted the wrong person, he could ruin their lives and put them in danger.

That was a lot of pressure.

"Are you sure you want to tell him?" Lorcan asked softly, placing a hand on his left shoulder as he moved to his side and helped dry the dishes Rylee had already washed and placed on the draining rack.

Nodding, he thought seriously about the question. No matter how he twisted and turned it, he always returned to the same answer. "Yes. I want him in my life, and I think he needs us. He's already shown promise and I...I feel like he's one of us," Rylee explained, knowing Lorcan needed more than his gut feelings to judge this on. Emotions were fine, but they didn't offer security or give Lorcan something to believe in.

"Okay. We give him time to recover from this and you'll tell him," Lorcan agreed, spending the next few minutes focusing on the dishes he was drying. "Be honest, tell him how you feel. You can offer proof if he needs it, but stress there's a serious risk to us if he goes running his mouth," he suggested.

Yeah, it made sense. But it was hard. Rylee knew the odds of Drew freaking out and running. He'd never find him again.

Fuck it. What was life without a little risk?

*

It was late in the evening when Rylee returned to their bedroom, seeking sanctuary. He'd done a lot of thinking and soul searching as he wandered campus grounds, trying to decide if he should tell Drew the truth.

When he returned to the bedroom and found three of his fraternity brothers—Keon, Lorcan and Delaware—already there, he was stunned. Keon sat on his bed, running fingers through Drew's hair in a far too familiar way, while Lorcan and Delaware sat on Drew's untouched bed talking quietly.

"What's with the meeting?" Rylee asked teasingly, as he removed his jacket and laid it over the chair by the desk.

Keon sighed. "Drew's got the Fever," he revealed, still carding his fingers through his hair. He looked worried, as he explained why he thought Drew had such a deadly disease. "He was found wandering in the basement when Lorcan was preparing one of the cats. He secured the cat and brought Drew out, thinking he'd freak at seeing something he shouldn't have, when he started rambling. Drew kept asking to speak to me, but when I arrived, he said he'd made his decision."

"Decision?" he wondered, looking amongst the others for an explanation.

"Whether to stay or leave," Lorcan replied.

Interesting. Rylee believed Drew had already decided to stay, not because of their attraction, but it had been a factor in why he thought that wouldn't change. Hell, Drew had said they both weren't the type to sleep around, implying they were about to embark on a relationship. Which made Rylee believe he had to stick around.

"Granted, he's acting a little weird," he allowed, staying calm. "He's been exhausted for the past few days and he *is* going through something disorientating, but it's *not* the Fever, I can assure you. Drew isn't capable of going through the Fever," he warned, hoping to reassure them it wasn't possible.

Lorcan raised an eyebrow. "How do you know he doesn't have the Fever? Rylee, you know fine well anyone from Vihaan can get it," he complained, clearly thinking he'd lost his mind.

Rylee smiled and corrected them. "He's not *from* Vihaan," he said, crossing to tap Keon's shoulder. With a nod, telling him to move his caboose or have it moved, Rylee waited for Keon to shuffle over and took his place. He placed his hand on Drew's cheek and caressed the prominent cheekbone.

The bags under his eyes were more prominent than ever, emphasising how pale Drew had become. It was happening faster than he'd expected, but there was nothing Rylee could do to help but stay close and offer his support.

"Are you sure he's not from Vihaan?" Delaware asked quietly, as he bit the tip of his nail.

Rylee nodded and figured it was time to explain. "When I checked for the fifth stage, I found four scratches on his hip and three on his shoulders. When I used our link to investigate, I found out he's...he was with a guy about two years ago. He was..." He had to stop because thinking the name made him feel sick. "He was with Aniel."

Lorcan gasped and Keon frowned, while little innocent Delaware looked completely confused. "That makes no sense," Lorcan argued, walking over to place his hand on Rylee's shoulder. "What is Aniel doing outside of Vihaan? Why would he be with Drew? And what in the fucking hell would give him cause to mark him?" he asked, his voice growing louder and louder as he realised the implications of this news.

The way it had hit Rylee like a lead weight when he found out. "I don't know," he replied, figuring it would answer his questions. He tried not to notice how his voice shook or the effort it took to talk about the bastard again, but it needed to be done.

"I don't know what he did, how, or why," Rylee confessed quietly, stroking his fingers through Drew's hair. "What I saw was...cruel. He used Drew like a Vihaan whore." He couldn't help but bite the words out.

It made his skin crawl. Vihaan whores remained the lowest of society, no longer people but a mindless body seeking the next high. Worse than the drug addicts of this world, Vihaan whores were ruthless, attacking anyone who fed their desire for blood, sex and pain. Thinking about Drew being treated like trash hurt.

Rylee had to shake it off when he saw how worried the others looked. He was giving far too much away but couldn't care. "He hurt him and said the cruellest things, to degrade him and make him feel unworthy of being alive. He treated Drew like trash and discarded him as easily," he continued, hoping they understood how important this was. "He left him with a reminder of their relationship. Not just with the scars, but with the fear and mistrust he's carried around ever since. If you think what Drew's dad did was awful, imagine how he felt after Aniel told him it was true—he was worthless, useless and didn't deserve to live."

The room was silent in the wake of the revelation. Until Delaware spoke.

"Sorry, but who is Aniel?"

Rylee realised Delaware was too introverted to have found out the truth. He smiled to lessen the blow and replied, "The ex who left me to marry my sister."

Chapter Sixteen

Drew's mouth was stale and gummy, his eyes sticky. Waking in the middle of the night was bad enough without knowing he'd been asleep since the night before. His head throbbed as he turned to find Rylee lying beside him, one arm curled around his waist.

He was naked, something he wanted to fix.

Pushing Rylee's hand away, he shuffled to the bottom of the bed and wobbled as he attempted to stand on his own two feet. Clearly a whole day without food or water but plenty of sleep hadn't done him any good. It was time to remedy that, but first...he desperately wanted a shower.

Drew left the room and walked to the end of the corridor where there was a family bathroom, mostly used for guests or during parties, and slipped inside to grab a shower there. At least he'd avoid waking Rylee, even if it did mean forcing his tired body to move farther away from the bed to get there.

Once under the spray of chilled water, Drew tipped his head and basked in the delight of being clean and refreshed again. Though his mind was still foggy and his eyes tired, a blast of cold water helped alleviate the struggle to stay awake. It was glorious to feel the way the water trickled over his skin, even as it hissed and stung against skin which burned like fire.

When his eyes drooped, Drew left the shower and glanced at the towel, discarding the idea. He would drip dry as he walked to the bedroom. Maybe it would help him cool down. All he wanted was to go back to the room, climb aboard Rylee and fuck his way through the exhaustion plaguing his mind.

Passing by the other rooms between Rylee's and the bathroom, he was surprised to hear his name being mentioned. Moving closer, he pressed his ear to the door and recognised Delaware's voice claiming Drew had something call *the Fever* and he was acting irrationally. Which seemed rude coming from the sweet guy.

Still, maybe the Fever was part of their BDSM code for something else. Like being horny.

Drew walked straight to Rylee's room and shut the door behind him, finally free to crawl onto the bed. His plan to climb the delicious pogo stick—he stopped as the phrase caught on his brain and he giggled at how ridiculous it sounded. When Rylee moaned, he pressed his lips together to suppress the sound and changed his plans.

Pulling off the covers, he revelled in the sight of Rylee, naked, his dick already half hard. He must have been having a nice dream. Drew wanted to share it with him, to give his dream the *happy ending* a great guy like Rylee deserved.

He wrapped his lips around the head of his long cock and nudged forwards to take a little more into his mouth. Humming at the bitter taste of precome as it dropped onto his tongue. Drew was about to back off and lick every inch of the length when a hand caught the back of his head and Rylee's hips rose off the bed, shoving his full length into Drew's mouth.

Swallowing the offering the best he could, he alternated the deep thrusts with a swirl of his tongue around the slit, backing off enough to breathe.

"Drew," Rylee whispered, gripping his hair tighter as his hips sped up, pumping his cock in and out of his mouth. It bordered on too much until Rylee gasped and his hips froze, his hand released Drew's hair as he was pushed away. "Drew? What the fuck?"

Sitting back on his heels, Drew wiped his mouth. Careful of where he placed his hands, he crawled over Rylee and kissed his lips. "Will you fuck me, Rylee? Please?" he asked, using his right hand to caress his gorgeously hairy chest. He tugged on a few hairs, watching Rylee grit his teeth. Drew ducked and kissed his way from one nipple to the other. "Please," he whispered.

For maybe five minutes, Rylee gripped his waist and shuddered under his ministrations.

"Please," he repeated, sucking a pert nipple into his mouth. "I got to fuck you. Now, I want you to fuck me," he reasoned, remembering the night Rylee pleaded with him to wake so Rylee could bottom. He'd never thought Rylee was the type to switch it up, but Drew hadn't minded.

With a groan, Rylee grabbed his arms and pushed Drew onto the bed, pressing him into the mattress in a way he hoped promised more to come. Those pretty eyes bore into him as the tight line of his mouth opened and said, "No."

"Why not?"

"Because you're not yourself." Rylee moved contrary to Drew's hopes, leaving the bed and dressing. As Drew opened his mouth to argue, Rylee returned to offer a kiss of compromise. "I'm going to get you a special tea. It will take your temperature down. Try to sleep or wait for me here. Don't leave the room." Drew was still searching for words when he realised Rylee was gone.

*

Not sure what was happening or why, Drew refused to wait around and be rejected again. If he wasn't going to get a decent lay, he may as well investigate. A tickle in the back of his brain told him he was looking for something. He couldn't think what it was, but he'd know when he saw it.

First, he wanted to explore the strange mark in Rylee's bedroom ceiling. Drew grabbed the bedside table, shoved it into the middle of the room and climbed on top of it. Though he wobbled once both feet were on the surface, he was able to reach the mark in the ceiling and push. As he'd suspected, a hatch opened.

Drew frowned at the darkness above and reached with his right hand to search the flooring of the room above—an attic?—for a light switch. His hand hit something hard which fell over with a bang.

Hot hands clamped over his wrist, his startled scream nothing more than a croak in his dry mouth. Beyond any reasonable strength, those arms managed to lift him off his feet, leaving him dangling in midair, held by two hands which didn't leave the darkness of the attic's shadows.

"What the fuck are you?" he shouted, scrambling with his left hand to fight against whatever had a hold of him.

The bedroom door banged open, drawing Drew's panicked gaze to where Lorcan stood with a baseball bat. When he saw what was happening, he dropped the bat and pushed the bedside table out from under Drew's feet.

"What are you doing?" he shouted, knowing he needed it below his feet if he was going to get down.

"Let Drew go," Lorcan spoke casually, calmly. It didn't fit the situation. Nor did the loosening grip which dropped Drew, landing him on his backside.

He couldn't smother his scream as he backed into the corner of the room. "What the fuck is going on?"

While Lorcan watched with sad eyes, Drew kept hidden in the corner of the room, out of reach from the monster in the attic. He wanted answers as to what it was, why it was in the attic, and why the fuck Rylee had direct access to it. Then he'd want answers about the seriously fucked state of things concerning the illegal trading of exotic animals, this talk about the Fever and why he had been unable to stay awake for three days.

After a few minutes, Lorcan took a step and a blink made his eyes flicker between a round human iris to something inhumanly shaped, long and thin. Drew rushed to his feet and pressed into the wall, while screaming, "Stay the fuck away from me!"

Lorcan flinched as a crowd gathered outside the room.

No one moved. Not until Rylee pushed past them to stand behind Lorcan in the doorway. "Shit," he muttered, an understatement in this situation.

His entire body shaking from fear and the instinct to run, Drew managed to take a step. "Rylee, you better start fucking talking, or I'll scream the place down. I want to know what the fuck that is," he said, pointing to the ceiling, "and I want a clear answer to my questions. I can't take this shit anymore. I'm used to feeling like a complete fuck-up and hating myself for betraying you, but I won't be treated like a moron and not know if I'm safe in this house."

Rylee looked to Lorcan, growling out, "What the fuck is he talking about?"

"He met Malachi."

Met? Drew didn't want to know what it was he'd "met". He wanted the truth. In the state he was in—and perhaps they were right about the fever—one truth deserved another.

Stepping forwards, he raked his trembling hand through his hair. "I was kicked out years ago, Rylee. I came here as a favour to my brother, because he's a cop, investigating an illegal smuggling ring he believes is operating out of this house, selling exotic animals on the black market," he revealed, watching the shock pass over the many faces staring at him. Worst was the look of hurt flickering over Rylee's eyes. "Because of my background and being gay, my brother sent me in to investigate, after you scared off or caught his previous undercover cops," he continued, choosing not to look at anyone but Rylee.

"You know how much I hate my family. I wanted to earn the money and get out of this place. I wanted to escape my life. To get as far away from their poison as I could, and I needed money," he explained, hoping Rylee understood. "I didn't know I'd feel at home here. You guys are like me...lost and alone in the world. I didn't know I could make friends without wondering if my father had paid them to get close to me. I didn't know I could help people without being afraid it was part of my brother's plans to have me tied into a legal case for two years, until I couldn't escape."

Drew knew he was rambling and confessing too much when he caught the compassionate look Keon gave him from the doorway, as though he understood everything. He didn't care. Only one truth mattered, and he cried as he said it.

"My entire life has been a fucking failure. One abusive boyfriend after another, working for my father or paid to be with me and keep me in the shadows to make sure I can't tarnish his career, as he's about to make a big deal," he said, feeling nothing but pain as he thought back on those times. The guy who spelled it out for him was nothing more than a gay-for-pay job, because his father was afraid Drew couldn't stay away from the clubs long enough for his latest deal to be finalised.

He had to press his hands to his forehead as he remembered how horrible it had been. Sobbing and hiding in his bed for days afterwards. It wasn't anything compared to when Aniel dumped him and sent a video of their last time together to the press. They'd had a field day taking stills of Drew with tears in his eyes and a cock shoved in his mouth, talking about his *wild* and *depraved* ways, without realising the night had been closer to rape than anything he'd ever experienced. The night they laughed over and made jokes about had given him nightmares and had him too scared to even look another man in the eye for almost a year.

Tears slipped down his cheeks unchecked. Drew tried his best to ignore them and hold his head high, but he couldn't stand the look of pity in the half dozen pairs of eyes staring at him.

"I'm sorry. I've been holding off Sheffield as long as I can, but...I can't do this anymore," he confessed, feeling his entire body spasm. He had to hunch over his stomach to make it stop hurting. "I wanted...to love you...and have a home aga—"

He wanted to say he should leave; he would go willingly. A scream escaped instead. He had hurt too many people to stay, but his stomach twisted and hurt too much to get the words out.

In the distance, he could hear voices muttering about the Fever and someone saying they had to call the doctor. Someone let loose a stream of inventive swear words, most of which Drew didn't recognise. If he wasn't mistaken, it sounded like Lorcan.

"FUCK!" Drew screamed again, as something happened to his right leg which hurt like a bitch and brought him to his knees.

His last thought as he passed out was of how sorry he was for the pain in Rylee's eyes. If he could have said or done anything to take it away, he wished he'd thought of it before he blacked out.

Chapter Seventeen

At three o'clock in the morning, Rylee gathered the entire house into the meeting room downstairs and left Drew in the capable hands of their Vihaan doctor, Mister Robell.

"Quiet, please!" he called, as the room erupted in whispers and mutters asking why they'd been dragged out of their beds and had woken to Drew's screams. "If you'll shut up, I'll explain everything." He had to raise his voice to be heard, but the room dialled it down as soon as they heard his promise. "I'll start, and I'm going to ask Lorcan to explain the bit I was absent for, then I'll take over again, clear?"

He waited for a few head nods and grumbles of agreement. "I woke up not long ago with Drew's lips wrapped around my dick," he admitted, not caring how it sounded or about the chuckles following his words. He was being honest to the point of embarrassment. "Once I realised he was completely out of it and burning up, I shoved him off and had to let him down gently. I left the room to grab herbs from the garden. I was going to make him a tonic to bring his temperature down. When I got back, the whole fucking house was in chaos," he explained, gesturing for Lorcan to take over.

Lorcan nodded to the gathered boys. "Since my room is right next to Rylee's, I saw him leave. When I heard scraping, I thought Drew might need something, but with him vulnerable and a new cat in the house, I had to be careful. I went to investigate. I found him dangling from the ceiling with the bedside table beneath his feet. It seems he'd been snooping and found Malachi," he revealed, a few mutterings following his words. Everyone knew Malachi was kept secret for a reason.

Rylee didn't delve into it right now, since it was explained to new Vihaan recruits the minute they arrived. He'd explain the truth to Drew later, once he was feeling clearer. "When I got back," he said, taking over again, "Drew was screaming for answers and didn't want anyone near him. I guess he'd figured shit out on his own, but I'll explain the rest once he's feeling better," he admitted.

"What is important is what Drew said to those of us there to hear it for ourselves," he continued, worried about how this news would be received. Though it was true Drew had lied and attempted to deceive them, they had done the same. "Drew explained he's here undercover, working for his brother, who is a policeman. He's here to investigate the same exotic animal smuggling ring as the previous undercover officers. Drew was picked because he's not a cop, he's got experience working with wild animals and he's gay. He didn't have to fake it like the undercover cops did," he clarified.

"Attempted to," Martim muttered to his boyfriend, who sat next to him.

It was hard for Rylee to hide his grin. The poor guy had hit on the first undercover cop and immediately exposed him for what he was when an innocently stolen kiss had the cop freaking out and breaking cover to admit he wasn't gay.

Keon was the first to raise his hand, a common practice during meetings meant to sustain calm discussion and order.

"Keon?"

"Um, is that it?" he asked, looking around the room and standing from his seat. "I mean, I heard what Drew said. He agreed to come here because his brother was paying him and the money could go towards his escape from his family. I know how he feels. I came here to escape my family, in the same way Drew did. We have to accept their money and influence in our lives, but we do it to stay safe and maintain whatever degree of freedom we can," he said, wearing his heart on his sleeve.

Rylee couldn't have been prouder of him for saying it to the group. "I know, Keon. I get it," he promised, because he did see where Drew was coming from. "I completely agree Drew is not a threat to us. He admitted he'd been protecting us by lying to his brother, and from the way he came back from their lunch together, I can see it's hard on him. We don't have a lot of time. His brother will send someone to retrieve Drew or replace him soon."

That much he knew. It was a matter of time before Drew's brother figured out he was being railroaded. Once it happened, they were in trouble.

"I need to ask you to keep your cats under control until we can figure this out," he asked, hating it had to be done, but knowing it was for the best. "Drew has protected us, even in the midst of what he's been going through. The least we can do is make it easier for him to lie to his brother. We'll need to keep ourselves contained, keep our cats out of sight, and gut the house from top to bottom. Make sure no evidence exists to be used against us, got it?"

A round of "yes" and "sure" resounded throughout the room. Lorcan stepped forwards and offered Rylee a nod to say he'd take the floor. "I want to add one final note. Drew made his confession in tears. He said he wanted to escape his family. Like Keon said, it's a sentiment we understand," he began, sweeping his gaze around the room. "He said he'd found a home here. He wanted to love...us...and have a home here. I want to begin a motion to let Drew stay, for as long as he wants," he announced, raising his hand in a way asking for others to do the same if they agreed.

Rylee immediately added his hand, almost at the same moment Keon did. Delaware followed and it became a sea of hands rising into the air in agreement with Lorcan's request. He almost teared up to see the faith and loyalty his friends offered Drew freely. In the same way they'd rescued Malachi from a life of loneliness and pain, they banded together to protect Drew.

*

Drew woke to darkness and a lingering but muted pain which made his stomach twist as though he was about to be sick. Though he wanted to run to the bathroom, his entire body was leaden as though it had been strapped down.

"Rylee?" he managed, feeling parched and hoarse for no reason he could understand.

"Go fetch him," an unfamiliar voice said in the background of his thoughts. "Rylee will be here soon, Drew. I'm Doctor Robell and I'll be treating you for the duration of your transition," he explained, running a wet cloth over his forehead.

Frowning over the last word, he licked his lips and tried to speak, but he managed, "Sick."

The doctor pressed a hand to his left shoulder and carefully tipped him onto his side. The movement alone caused him to bypass any attempts at being civil or polite. He had no choice but to vomit the minute he was on his side. When he managed to force his eyes open—when had they shut again?—he saw a bucket held beneath him. He wanted to thank the quick-thinking Doctor, but the sight of the bloody vomit he'd brought up urged more out of his mouth.

"It's okay, Drew. This is natural in your situation," the man soothed, holding the bucket with one hand, while holding his hair with the other. "Try to breathe steadily and it will pass. I would give you a tea to keep your temperature down, but it will make you vomit more, I'm afraid. Best to get it out now, and then we can focus on getting you better afterwards."

The words were both sensible and calm, two things he needed right now. Drew managed to release the bed from his death grip—another thing he couldn't remember doing—and grab the doctor's wrist as he croaked out, "Thank you."

"You're welcome." The doctor chuckled. "I believe you met Malachi tonight. I'm sorry for the circumstances, but the boy doesn't like to be woken in the middle of the night or to have unexpected guests shoving their hands through his door. I'm sure you can understand, if not the violence of his reaction."

"Sure," Drew whispered, finding it easier on his throat. He did feel better since being sick. "Back?" he asked, frustrated he still couldn't form a cohesive sentence.

"Of course." Doctor Robell helped him roll onto his back and pressed the wet cloth to his forehead again. "I shall have another one ready to clean you up if you're sure you won't be sick again?" he offered, a hint of an accent in his voice.

Drew pressed his hand to the wet cloth on his forehead, enjoying the cold sensation it spread throughout his burning skin. "Thanks," he managed.

The doctor disappeared from his side and walked into the bathroom with another light chuckle. Drew didn't know what he found funny, but at least he was a nice guy and wasn't shouting like the doctors his father had made him visit. If it wasn't for feeling sick, he'd have found this whole mess peaceful.

After a few minutes, the doctor was at his side with another facecloth which he helped Drew use to clean his mouth. Almost the minute they were done, Rylee walked through the door and crossed to sink onto the bed by Drew's hip.

"Are you okay? Can I get you anything?" he asked, his eyes sad and his tone panicked.

Whatever had happened had sent everyone into a tailspin. "What...happened?" he asked, angry those words pushed aside the million questions he wanted to ask.

Rylee turned to frown at the doctor. "What the hell is wrong with him?"

Drew followed his worried gaze to Doctor Robell, but he didn't appear worried, smiling at Rylee as he replied.

"Nothing. His body and mind have suffered shock, due to the extreme transition he's undergone over the last week." The doctor pulled off his glasses and rubbed the lenses with the bottom of his shirt, the same way Drew did whenever he had to wear his reading glasses. "In an hour or two, his speech and movement will be back to normal. Or, rather, normal for a newborn of his kind. As his maker is not present, would you like me to run through the explanations or would you like to take care of it yourself?" he asked, not making a lick of sense to Drew's mind.

Maker? Why did it sound like a horrible science fiction, vampire novel? Had he undergone a modern-day Frankenstein's monster transformation?

"Wha—" Drew gritted his teeth when nothing else would come out. Now, he couldn't finish one damned word? Rylee dared to shush him like he was a baby. Too angry to speak and knowing he wouldn't get the right words out anyway, he grabbed the wet cloth from his forehead and threw it at Rylee's face. It hit with an awfully satisfying wet slap. Because, of the things that had happened since he woke, the cloth hit his target and got Rylee bullseye on his face.

When his boyfriend dragged it off and blinked in shock, Drew arched an eyebrow and reminded him he wasn't a moron. He was still in the damned room. He could hear and see them, he just couldn't communicate clearly yet.

"Sorry," Rylee said, with enough remorse Drew believed him. "Thank you for what you've done, Doctor Robell. I'll take it from here and call you tomorrow morning, when you can check him over again," he decided, speaking to the doctor while eyeing Drew carefully.

Feeling like a terrified child, but unable to show it, he waited as Rylee walked the doctor out of the room and said goodbye. By the time he'd returned, Drew had enough will to say, "Talk."

Chapter Eighteen

Rylee ran both hands over his face as he sank onto the seat the doctor had vacated, while Drew waited to find out what had happened. If it hadn't knocked him sideways, he would have waited to give Rylee time to breathe. But he was currently without a functioning voice, lacking appropriate movement abilities, and his brain acted like it had been freeze-dried and shoved in an oven to burn.

"Okay," Rylee said, eventually. He dropped his hands into his lap, took a deep breath and met Drew's gaze. "I have a lot to tell you and most of it needs to be explained. Will you promise not to interrupt?" he asked, scared and serious.He nodded.

His boyfriend gave him a short nod in return, then began to talk, "When you first arrived, we had an instant connection."

Drew broke his promise immediately, lifting his hand and pointing to his eye, because he couldn't currently wrap his tongue around the three-letter word. Somehow, he managed to murmur, "Red."

Rylee's eyes widened and he shuffled forwards on the seat. "You saw my eyes flash red?" he asked, letting loose a chuckle when Drew nodded. "Okay. That's amazing." Running his hand over his mouth, he began again, showing much more excitement. "Yes, I saw yours flash too. I'll explain later. What's important is I wasn't ready. I mean, it doesn't happen between two people every day.

It's something special. And I'm still a bit messed up from my last boyfriend, and I didn't want to jump right into something which had the potential to be serious.

"I couldn't help but flirt with you, to test the waters and find out if I'd imagined it. When you looked at me the way you did, I knew it wasn't a fluke. But you were shy and scared. I decided to keep you at arms-length. It didn't mean I had to keep my hands off my own dick," he confessed, smiling as he talked about it. "I had to do something, because you hit me like a freight train. Your scent is like...it's catnip to me, Drew. The minute I sniffed you in the doorway, I was hard as a rock and desperate to touch you. You have no idea how hard it was to restrain myself.

"But, you were new and had this sad story. Something told me jumping you on your first night was a terrible idea," he admitted, quirking an eyebrow as if to say *'see how it turned out.'* "You didn't make it easy on me, baby. You kept getting in my face, letting me smell you, making me watch you. You were in my bed at one point. I know, because it smelled like you when I went to sleep."

Drew almost laughed as he remembered. He bit his bottom lip and tried to figure out how to explain. Using both hands, he managed to form a *K*, which would be the best explanation.

"Keon?" Rylee guessed.

Nodding, he reached down to pinch the sheet covering his naked body and mimicked folding it.

Rylee dropped his face in his hand while shaking his head. "You helped him with the laundry?" he guessed, waiting for Drew's nod and barked out another laugh. "I thought you'd been a dirty bastard and jacked off in my bed!"

Since it hurt to talk, Drew offered a smile. He had to play the guessing game again, to get his point across. He touched his finger to his forehead, dragged it up and drew a pretend bubble.

"You wish, huh?" Rylee realised, smirking as he leaned in to kiss Drew's cheek. "I liked the thought of it too. I tried jacking off to relieve the pressure, but there was too much space between us it didn't feel right. I ended up getting out of bed and sitting beside you while you slept so I could jack off and sleep," he confessed, his cheeks flushing.

It was nice to hear his smell did that, even if the words sounded strange in his head. He couldn't be angry, since he'd succumbed to the same addictive attraction. Drew grabbed Rylee's hand and drew it to his lips, to kiss the palm, the only ability he had right now.

Rylee cleared his throat and shook his head. "Anyway, it was intense right from the start, and I didn't know what to do. I'd get jealous when you spent time with Keon, but you'd always look at me like I was a triple chocolate muffin waiting to be devoured. I couldn't get enough of it," he said, linking his fingers with Drew's. "I wanted to tell you how badly I wanted you, but I was scared of what could happen. I always chickened out. I was sure you knew about Vihaan, because one of your parents came from there." Which finally touched upon something Drew wanted to know more about. What was Vihaan exactly and why did no one want to talk about it?

Rylee took another deep breath and let it out slowly. "Vihaan is..." His words drifted into the ether, along with his distant gaze.

"Cult?" he managed, though it hurt, and he had to press his fingers to his throat to ease the pain after saying it.

"No, baby. Not a cult, though I can see why you'd think that," Rylee replied.

"Pict—"

"Pictures?" Rylee asked, frowning as though he didn't understand the connection between those two things.

Drew had to confess, to deserve an explanation from Rylee. He pointed to the wardrobe, made the shape of a USB with his fingers and mimicked plugging it in and clicking a mouse.

"Oh." Rylee's eyes widened briefly, and the frown returned. "You found my USB and saw the pictures?" he asked, and once Drew nodded, he licked his lips and asked, "Did you read my journal?"

He raised a finger, pointed to Rylee's heart and didn't know how to explain he knew he was heartbroken. He lay there, patting his heart and nodded, pulling Rylee's hand to his heart. He wanted to say "you're like me", "we've both been hurt" and "I know you're scared", but the words weren't there.

"Baby, I'm not sure what you mean, but I think it's beautiful." Rylee reached out to brush a strand of hair from his eyes. "Whatever you read, you're still here. It couldn't be too frightening for you. I guess, if it's about my heart then you read about how scared I was to be with you?"

Drew nodded and shrugged, not sure how to say it was okay, he understood and he didn't think it was bad.

Rylee seemed to know, regardless of what he did or didn't say. "Since you saw the photographs, it should be easier for you to understand Vihaan. You see, there's a kind of door between this world and Vihaan. A door which mixes things up when you walk through it. On Vihaan, I don't look like this. I look like...well, a tiger."

Narrowing his eyes, Drew began to question if he was still hallucinating. Or perhaps his hearing had been messed with as well as his speech? Until things clicked into place. "Cat," he said, again having to rub his throat because it hurt to make sounds.

With an eager nod, Rylee shuffled closer and cupped his cheek. "Yes, cat. We're cats. We come from a village within Vihaan called *Gheva Tarlou*, which roughly translates from the old Vihaanian into *Land of Cats*," he revealed, his nose wrinkling as he chuckled. "I know it's not original, but nothing on Vihaan is. I don't suppose you've ever seen the film *Bedknobs and Broomsticks*?"

Drew nodded once.

"It's like the *Isle of Naboombu*."

Wasn't that weird to hear from the mouth of a man nearly thirty years old. Drew shook his head and tapped his throat, wondering why, if this Vihaan was similar—and he knew the animals in the movie could talk—his voice was jacked up like a sledgehammer had hit it.

"It's the transitional process," Rylee soothed, cupping his cheek with a faint smile. "Like the doctor said, it will be fine in a little while. I was panicking at the time and forgot, but it's normal for those who have been...infected sounds wrong, but it's the best way to say it," he admitted, with a hint of apology.

Still not sure he was getting it, Drew pointed to himself and forced out another painful, "Cat?"

"Yes," Rylee confirmed, squeezing his hand. "Give me a few more minutes, and it should start to make sense, okay?"

What was Drew supposed to say? He didn't have much of a choice but to hear him out and try to figure out if Rylee had gone cuckoo or if Drew was the one already strapped in a psych ward, imagining this.

"Vihaan is like a world where animals talk. We're still animals. I mean, we don't walk on two feet or eat with a knife and fork. We're...like the *Jungle Book*."

Drew groaned and immediately regretted it. Rylee laughed. "I'm sorry. I know, another kid's movie. But the animations get it right sometimes," he claimed with a shrug. "Anyway, picture Vihaan like a beautiful world full of colour and scents and sounds, rich with life. Instead of humans, it's—"

"Jgl ook," Drew muttered, not sure what annoyed him more, not getting the words right or the fact he was talking about the *Jungle Book* being real.

"Right." The damned annoying smirk returned, while Rylee eyed him with amusement. "Vihaan has few laws or rules. You don't hookup with anyone—your own species or not—unless it's to have kids. There's no sex-for-pleasure on Vihaan, which means the law fucks those of us with same-sex inclinations, since there can't be any kids between us." He shrugged, his smile slipping.

"Those of us who are at risk of breaking the law wait until we're of age and escape to this world, where it's safer for us to be ourselves. The price is high. Coming through the door means leaving our cat behind. Physically, at least. Because, the minute we step through we're a human and it's like we share our human mind with the cat we were in Vihaan. We...split, coming through the door," he explained, struggling to find the right terms in a way Drew finally understood.

How could you explain something you'd only ever felt?

Drew squeezed Rylee's hand until Rylee met his gaze.

"We're not all animals though. I mean, Keon is half-animal, a bit like one of your werewolves, from those stories. He can choose to be his wolf or he can choose to be his human. He's both equally," he continued thoughtfully. "It would be nice to go between both, but my people can't. We're purely animals until we cross into this world. Unfortunately, our DNA and our hair still register as animal to tests. We can't visit regular doctors or hospitals if we get injured. It's why we have a whole host of medical supplies in the shed," he elaborated quietly.

Drew wanted to smack himself stupid. He assumed the shed was where they kept the wild cats, but it was a medical storage facility. With how big it was, there was probably a makeshift operating table in there, for when they had accidents requiring surgery or copious blood loss. They couldn't exactly do it in the frat house, could they?

As he was mentally berating his stupidity, Rylee kept talking. "We can't go back. It's what makes the decision harder for those of us from *Gheva Tarlou*. Keon's people, from a village called *E'Boolou*, can pass between both worlds freely. They can make themselves appear human at will. There's less danger to them. For us, coming through is a bit like having our DNA ripped out of us and someone using it to lock us out forever. Even if we changed our minds after realising we'd become fully human, there's no going back. Ever."

Drew wished he could console Rylee, but he held his hand and listened. He'd accepted his words as the truth somewhere along the way, perhaps because of the true passion and the sadness in Rylee's eyes as he spoke of his homeland. Whatever it was, Drew believed him and trusted he wasn't in danger.

"Brother?" he asked, feeling less scratch and resist from his voice as he attempted to speak.

Rylee frowned and it took him a moment for realisation to hit. "Your brother? You're worried about what Sheffield will do to us?" he asked, and though it wasn't exactly what he'd meant, it suited his purpose. Drew nodded. "Your brother can't do anything, baby. If they take us in for testing, they'll get fucked results they'll blame on a mistake in the lab. They can't arrest us without proof," he soothed, as though it solved everything.

But it didn't.

Pressing his fingers to his throat and wondering when the healing would begin, Drew shook his head and pointed to the wardrobe again, then below the floor. Sheffield wouldn't need proof if the cops found the photographs and their dungeon room. That would be it, they'd be charged and convicted of animal smuggling and imprisoned, because the photos proved they had wild animals in a fraternity without a license and the dungeon room would corroborate the photographs, giving the cops a valid location to match the photographs to.

His damned stupid mouth wouldn't say the words.

"I'm sorry, baby. I don't know what you mean."

Struggling past the pain, he bit out, "Dungeon!" It came out with a roar far too primal to be natural. Wide-eyed, Drew stared at Rylee as the wheels began turning and locking into place.

"Yeah, I guess I need to explain, huh?"

Chapter Nineteen

Drew narrowed his eyes as Rylee stood from his seat, disappeared into the bathroom and returned with a cup of water.

"If you can keep this down, I'll make you a herbal tea to help with the fever and the pain," he promised, retaking his seat to offer the cup. He didn't make Drew take it, he tipped it against his lips and allowed him to decide how much he wanted.

When he was done, he tapped the back of Rylee's hand and sighed.

"Right, first...the dungeon," he continued calmly.

Drew wished he had another projectile to throw.

"It's not a dungeon, for a start. It's a reconditioning room. You see, the people who come through can be a little fucked up. The likes of Keon, who can change at will, can't always control the shift when they come through from Vihaan. The stress is too much and they can't remain mentally aware of who they are and what they're doing here," he explained, sounding like he was choosing his words carefully.

"They would be a danger to themselves, the entire house, and anyone they came across in the outside world. We isolate them for their own good," Rylee elaborated. "For a few days, I'm the only one who visits them, because I'm the strongest. Even in human form. I go in, have a chat with them and try to reason with their higher functioning brain. Mostly they're snarling beasts, not able to talk or move much," he went on.

With a bob of his head, Rylee made an uncertain face. "I guess they're like you. For them, it's more intense because they don't know they *should* be talking or moving. They don't know I'm trying to help them," he said, reaching out to trail his finger over the back of Drew's hand. "It takes about a week for them to change into a human again. They're kept there, because they're the most basic human, the most basic of animals. Once they can show clear memories and act as they should, they're let out and allowed another week within the basement to adjust.

"Rarely, we'll have Vihaan come to us months or years after coming to this world, because their human life is too stressful. They want to be an animal for a while or it's become too much and they can't control their shift," Rylee continued calmly. "We offer them a safe place. Whatever they need. In return, they help out around the house when they can or they offer advice, once they're ready to go home, to the younger or newer recruits. They show them there's the chance to have a real life here, even if it gets hard."

Stopping to take a breath, Rylee grasped Drew's hand in both of his and met his gaze with beautiful big eyes that said how sorry he was. "On the other matter, yes. You are becoming one of us. No, I didn't do this to you. Not really," he concluded.

Not really didn't tell Drew much, but it was enough to suggest there was more. He gestured with his hand for Rylee to continue. He wanted to hear it, to decide what he was going to do next.

"Your ex-boyfriend from two years ago," he said, making Drew flinch. He shouldn't know about Aniel.

"We'll come back to him. Sorry. First, the minute we met we sparked a chain reaction called *M'Nuni* or "the Mating" back home," he continued, his eyes twinkling with mischief. "The Mating can't be recognised until all five steps are completed by the turn of a new moon. We saw the red flash, we kissed, I topped you and you topped me. Step five wasn't my doing, but the rest were."

Drew looked away as he thought about it. He hadn't explained what step five was and, apparently, someone other than his boyfriend had completed it. "What?" he managed, finding it easier to get out those hard sounds.

"Step five is the mark. Someone from Vihaan must mark you to complete the process. It can be done before, during, or after the other steps. Yours happened before," Rylee revealed, too sad to make sense. "Every time we completed a step, our mental connection grew. We began to share thoughts and memories. Such as when you thought you "remembered" me calling you "the sexiest little kitten". You plucked the words right out of my thoughts. Later, I looked into your memories to find out who marked you. It was done two years ago, on your last night with Aniel. The night he..." He stopped and Drew didn't have to ask why.

He averted his gaze, realising Rylee had witnessed the events of that night. He didn't want to talk about it. Now or ever.

Thankfully, Rylee cleared his throat and avoided saying what they both knew. "I recognised Aniel, because he's the man I was going to spend my life with in Vihaan. Or, rather, the tiger I had given myself to. The man who married my sister."

*

For a long time after Rylee said the words, the room remained silent. The other boys had gone to their beds, but there was no way Drew could sleep now. Not knowing his ex—the vindictive, vicious bastard he was—had been the man who broke Rylee's heart.

Was that all Aniel could do? Break hearts and hurt people?

What a cruel twist of fate it was to bring two of his victims together. Or was it more than a coincidence? Was it part of Aniel's plan or was it merely the truth of how far Aniel's evil could spread?

"Rylee," he said, feeling stronger now he'd had time to rest and think it over. As soon as Rylee met his gaze, Drew squeezed the hand holding his and struggled to move back on the bed, to make room for one more body. "Stay?"

Rylee smiled, sad and lost, as he left his seat and slipped onto the bed beside Drew. "I'm sorry to throw this at you at once. I hoped we'd have more time, and I could ease you into this. I knew how hard it would be for you to swallow the thought we're pretty much animals at heart," he confessed, his voice heavy with emotion Drew wished he could take away. Regret, self-hate, frustration, it was there in his voice.

"Makes...sense..." Drew admitted, while struggling to do the same. "Cats...every...where. Cat smell. Cat talk. Cat jokes," he continued, grinning as he realised he was beginning to get more words out and, considering cat had an awfully hard *K* sound, his voice must have been getting better.

Rylee chuckled quietly, but didn't try to correct his pathetic attempt at sentences. "True. We're a little obvious, aren't we?"

"Sheff...ield will know," he managed, taking it a little bit at a time. "Smart and not...nice. He...won't care if...you're nice." Drew swallowed and shifted to lay his head on Rylee's shoulder, trying to take comfort from knowing, no matter what he was going through, he wouldn't be doing it alone. "It'll make...no...diff...erence," he continued, breaking the words into manageable parts to say what he needed to say, "if I'm cat."

Damn it. He hated how it sounded, but it was the best he could do.

Rylee lifted his hand and pressed his thumb lightly to Drew's Adam's apple, slowly stroking the area and running his fingertips over the skin in a light caress. "Yeah, I was afraid of that. But we don't have any choice. We can't move. Everyone in Vihaan knows to come here if they want to escape and, if I leave, Vihaan's are going to appear at their wildest moment," he complained, clearly frustrated with the idea.

Drew understood why. The Vihaan's who came through the doorway unstable would have no safe haven left, no one to understand what was happening. Showing up as wild beasts at a random human's door.

"Need to give...alternative," he realised, as it was all they had left. "Throw...bus."

Crap.

"Throw...bus?" Rylee repeated with a curious, questioning tone. "Throw a bus? No, that makes no sense. Throw under the bus?" He sounded pleased and looked down, as Drew nodded. Exactly what he'd meant to say. "Throw someone else under the bus? To save the house?" he guessed.

"Yes." It came out as more of a hiss than he'd have liked, but he could argue about it later if he had to. "Needs to arrest...s-s-someone. If S-S-Sheff-ield is happy, he will go away," he said, fighting for every word.

Rylee hummed and carded fingers through Drew's hair for a quiet moment. "We need to find someone to frame for this whole exotic animal smuggling ring your brother suspects us of having a part in, to protect the house and distract him."

"Aniel."Chuffing a threat of laughter, Rylee sounded like a tiger. Drew knew he was right to trust him. It was a crazy story, but it made sense of the small things he'd encountered and discovered since coming here.

"Aniel," he repeated, refusing to let Rylee pass it off as a joke. "He's...bad. Evil. And...cat. Bad history with...both of us. Show S-S-Sheff—" Unable to repeat his brother's damned infuriating name, he bypassed it completely. "Show cops Aniel is...f-framing you in...revenge," he explained, closing his eyes when he was done and praying his voice would get stronger the more he used it. He was sick of not being able to say what popped into his head without having to think it through first.

The silence which met his words wasn't exactly inspiring.

A soft sigh roused Drew as he was about to drift off to sleep. "How would we frame him? We'd have to prove beyond a reasonable doubt he was harbouring exotic animals."

He nodded and said the words which terrified him. "I'll go and...con-front him about...what he did...to me. Aniel will be angry and will...want to...hurt me. To keep me quiet," he admitted, meeting Rylee's uncertain eyes. "You will call...my brother. Tell him...I followed...a lead to Aniel. I went alone. He will come and...find Aniel with...cat. Me. Then...I escape." It was the best plan he could think of.

Rylee didn't look convinced, but it made sense. If Aniel was caught in possession of an exotic wild cat, he would be the perfect scapegoat for the business Sheffield thought Rylee and the house responsible for. The cops would believe Aniel framed them, trying to incriminate Rylee, and planted those cat hairs and whatever other circumstantial evidence they thought they had. Once the cat was caught, Drew would turn back to his human body and escape.

"No." Rylee caressed his cheek. "You can't go alone. If this is the only way, Keon should go with you. He can turn at will. Between now and then, he can teach you how to do it. But we need time to find Aniel and plan it to the last minute."

Drew began shaking his head. "Sheff-ield gave me...a fort-n-n-night. Lost two days...already," he argued, because they were running out of time. The cops would come bursting into the house and damage whoever—or whatever—they found. "Malachi," he added, to emphasise the danger.

If his brother and his men found Malachi, there was no telling what might happen.

"Right." Rylee's eyes went wide in recognition. "Malachi would be a problem. He's half insane from what happened. If they find him—" He didn't need to finish.

Drew kissed his cheek in apology. This wasn't how or when it should have happened, but he understood he'd given them little choice. Once he underwent his first true transformation, he risked losing his trust in this new family he'd found, forever. The secrets had to be spilled now.

Chapter Twenty

Rylee barely slept. He was too aware of Drew beside him. Every toss and turn, every sound that escaped him as he shifted in bed or dreamed had him wide awake and worrying over another bout of pain or sickness.

He fell asleep around six in the morning, waking to the clock reading 11:00 a.m. and an empty bed. Knowing Drew wasn't beside him was his first priority. Rylee jumped out of bed and checked the bathroom, then the house bathroom, wondering if he'd showered there to avoid waking him. When it revealed nothing, he raced downstairs and skidded to a halt to find Drew sitting at the breakfast table with the rest of the house, talking quietly with Keon.

"Morning, Rylee," Lorcan said from his seat at the side of the table. "Hungry?" he asked, offering a plate of bacon.

As instinct told him to grab a slice before they disappeared into ever-hungry mouths, Drew gasped and bounced out of his chair. "Rylee!" he cheered, rushing over to throw his arms around his waist.

He had never been greeted warmly or...well, with raw excitement. This wasn't the Drew he was used to. "Morning, baby," he said, trying to act natural while he dipped his head to kiss Drew's dark hair.

With a hum of delight, Drew held on tight and refused to let go. While Rylee searched for something to say or do in reaction to this strange behaviour, Drew rubbed his cheek against his T-shirt and heaved a satisfied sigh.

"You've never turned anyone, have you?" Martim asked, with a hint of realisation in his voice.

Rylee flushed against his better judgement. Martim had turned his boyfriend a year ago, after accidentally exposing the secret, and Doctor Robell advising him to either lose his boyfriend or bring him into the fold.

"Um, no." He patted Drew's shoulders awkwardly, realising they had walked into this venture blind. At least they'd learn together.

Martim rose from his seat to approach Drew. "You turned him, and he's connected to you on a much deeper level than the Mating. He *wants* to be with you. Right now, he's marking you as his and he'll expect you to mark him as yours," he warned, pressing his hands to Rylee's as they sat on Drew's shoulders. "You have to break him of the habit now. If you allow it, he'll worship you from dawn to dusk and never listen to another authority. If you break it now, you'll be protecting both of you in the long run. But it's not pleasant. You have to set goals, restrictions and try your hardest not to touch him in public. Touching can be the reward you give him for a day well spent when you're alone," he explained.

Drew pouted as though he didn't want to listen to those words and tightened his grip on Rylee's waist.

"Geez, baby. Loosen up a little," he complained, pushing his arms away until he could breathe. Checking with Martim, he questioned his ability to live countless days without touching Drew in any capacity. "Does it have to be completely hands-off?"

Martim shook his head, eyes full of amusement. "No. Make whatever rules you want, but you have to set them now and keep to them. A good concept is to compare him to a puppy who needs to be properly trained to become a well-behaved adult dog. It's something humans understand better than *do as you're told*." He shrugged and consulted his boyfriend, who grinned and nodded his agreement.

"Okay." Rylee contemplated it, as Drew blinked big blue eyes full of hope. "We'll figure out our own deal, okay? You need to sleep and rest. Nothing too taxing for at least twenty-four hours while we put our plan together," he decided.

Much like a puppy, Drew nodded, eager to please. Since he wasn't about to let go, Rylee cupped his ass and lifted him off his feet. Which, as he suspected, was exactly what his little kitten wanted, because he snuggled in and held on tight.

"Keon, could you bring a huge amount of food for us, please?" he asked, trusting Keon to know what Drew would like.

"Oooh!" Drew raised his head and blinked at Keon. "Can I have a *Red Blooded Male*?"

"Haven't you already got one?" Keon retaliated, earning a stuck-out tongue from Drew which he returned with one of his own. "I'll bring an entire buffet, don't you worry," he promised, laughing as Rylee headed for the staircase.

If he wasn't mistaken, Drew was acting more like a kid than a puppy. It was nice he and Keon got along well enough to exchange friendly banter. God knows, he'd need a good friend to turn to in the days to come, when he was too scared or too unsure of turning to ask for Rylee's help. Because Drew was a stubborn mule. How he liked him.

*

Once full of food, Drew started acting more like normal. He dialled down the constant need for contact by sitting between Rylee's legs and burrowing into his arms, rather than hanging off whatever limb he could attach to.

It made having Keon, Lorcan, and Delaware in their bedroom to help them discuss the future less awkward than it could have been. Still, Rylee wasn't ready to let go of Drew yet either. He was going through something huge and it was natural he'd want an anchor to keep him grounded.

At least he'd eaten a healthy portion. It had taken barely a few minutes for Drew to demand an explanation for why he was hungry when he normally had a minimal appetite.

"Your metabolism will be working at eight or nine times the rate it used to, to prepare for your second transformation," Rylee explained calmly, as he dug into his burger.

"First," Drew argued.

"Sorry, baby. Your first transformation was the reason you passed out and woke in bed," he apologised, the same way he did to new hybrids who had been turned and couldn't fathom why they lost a huge chunk of time from their memory. "Because you were surrounded by us—what your cat sees as your own kind—you turned and curled up to go to sleep, because you and your cat are safe," he elaborated, hoping talking it through helped Drew understand.

Rylee diverted the conversation to where it began. "Now you'll see why we eat a lot, especially in the morning. You'll be doing the same, from now on. And the food truck this stuff came from, it's run by a man from Vihaan. A lion who was once high in society until he got caught courting a warrior in the pride. He was banished here and started running the food truck for us lost Vihaan's," he explained, watching Drew for any sign this was too much.

He knew how frightening it could be to realise his body had changed. Hell, his first day as a human had been terrifying until he figured out what had happened and found clothes. After, it was a matter of letting his cat guide him to a human who smelled of cat. The man was in his eighties at the time, had met a cat who had been exiled, and had learned their secrets well enough to know what Rylee was by sight. He helped him get the right papers, the documentation, and important details of his life together.

He wished the cantankerous bastard hadn't died a year later, because he would have done a better job of easing Drew into this.

"Does he only serve Vihaan food?" Drew asked, snapping him out of the thought with an innocent look.

"Um, yeah. When he started the truck, humans never came. It was like he was invisible," Rylee explained, remembering how worried the man had been when they first met. "It was weird, but it seems the doorway between our worlds has a way of keeping us contained and safe. The man who taught me about the transition between worlds used to say Vihaan's never meet a human who isn't a guide or a potential mate. If we met a human by accident, the human was one of those things."

Drew smiled and leaned in to kiss his cheek. "It's a nice thought," he whispered, settling into Rylee's arms without another word.

He cleared his throat, remembering their audience lined up on Drew's bed. Or rather, what had been Drew's bed until they fell for each other. Though his friends were being suspiciously quiet, he'd thought it was to give Drew a chance to absorb what was being said, not because they were spying.

"Anyway...the guy discovered only Vihaan's or those going through the transformation can see his truck. No humans. We've been regular customers for years," Rylee rounded off. "The reason you saw it was because we'd already started the process," he explained, not sure how else to phrase it with such eagle-eyed company spying on them.

"Huh. There are a lot of Vihaan here then? More than the ones in this house?"

Rylee nodded and he hummed, barely surprised. Probably wondering if he would be able to tell the difference, now he was becoming one.

"Awesome. I love it. It makes me want to run," Drew admitted, taking a huge bite out of his burger and moaning obscenely.

At any other time, Rylee would have thought it was play-acting for their audience, but he knew the thrill of tasting Vihaan meat for the first time in an age and how it spoke to the cat within him. He didn't doubt Drew's cat was basking in the flavours. Hopefully, the food wasn't the only part of being a cat Drew liked.

Time would tell how he accepted this new change to his life. Rylee could only wait and hope for the best.

Chapter Twenty-One

Two Days Later

Four days of their fortnight had gone and Drew didn't feel any closer to being capable of making a second transformation. Without the ability, they could kiss their plan to frame Aniel goodbye.

Drew was still struggling to believe he was a mythical creature. If he couldn't believe it, then how could he convince anyone else? The deeper question was did he want to be a supernatural anomaly?

"Essentially, I'm a human who can turn into a cat," he repeated, for the sake of the lesson he was sitting through. Once again. With the same audience: Rylee, Lorcan, Delaware, and his new bestie, Keon.

"Yes. Which probably means it will take more out of you than normal if you want to become a cat. Do you know what kind you are?" Lorcan replied, yet again following an explanation with a question.

"There's more than one?"

Keon made a face, probably because he was the single lupine in a house of cats. "Lion, tiger, lynx, leopard..." He trailed off at the end with a gesture which said the list continued.

Drew nodded, realising the problem. "Oh. Don't I become what my maker was?" he asked, refusing to mention the bastard's name again. He'd already infiltrated Drew's life and his relationship with Rylee. He wasn't going to give him the satisfaction of having his name constantly rolling off their tongues.

"Actually, no. And we never saw what you became, because you burrowed under the blankets too quickly." Rylee leaned over his knees and shrugged. "No one knows how it happens, but the theory is some humans contain a special genetic marker. When it counteracts with the Vihaan genes through the scratches, it creates hybrid results unique to each human," he explained, with far too many technical terms for Drew to care about.

"No human is what their maker was? Or it's a roulette wheel with a 50/50 chance?" he wondered, trying to gauge how things would work out if he was something other than the tiger Rylee was. Since Rylee couldn't turn into his tiger anymore, he supposed it didn't matter in a physical sense, but what if his cat's scent turned Rylee off or repulsed him?

Delaware nibbled on his bottom lip and shrugged. "We don't see many cats turning humans. We can't say. Martim is the only one I know of and Doctor Robell recommended it. Trying to maintain a relationship between cat and human is hard, with the secrets we have to keep and the threat of human hunters," he admitted.

Drew blinked at his friend in surprise. "Human...hunters?"

Rylee raised his hand in a wait-a-minute gesture. "They are rare. They're generally human children with one Vihaan parent and one human parent. The genetic lottery judges whether they're a mix of both or one over the other. Often, when they're human, they see Vihaan's as a stain upon humanity," he explained, rolling his eyes at the phrase which must have been from the hunters.

"They seek out other humans like them, who know about Vihaan and our existence. They spend their lives hunting us and recruiting humans who don't have the keen senses the Vihaan offspring inherit from their parents."

"They have superpowers?"

Laughing, Keon threw a cushion at him. "The ungrateful bastards are born with their Vihaan parent's senses. The pricks choose to embrace those *differences* and use them against us, completely forgetting where they got them from. A human Vihaan offspring can look at a room full of people and pinpoint which one's have Vihaan blood," he warned, with a gravity he understood too well.

Drew now had Vihaan blood. He was now a target of these human hunters as soon as they crossed his path.

Hyperventilating took precedence over rational thought, and he couldn't see for the multitude of spots forming in front of his eyes. He wanted to run, to escape his life and this new discovery. To go back in time and never take this damned assignment. To tell Sheffield to go to Hell in a handbasket and take the whole family with him. But...he wouldn't have Keon as a best friend or Rylee as a boyfriend. And he wanted them in his life. It didn't change the fact he was stuck being something he'd never asked to be. Because Aniel had caught his eye in a club and been exciting enough to capture his interest. Later, he'd been too afraid to escape.

Everything narrowed to a single tunnel of darkness in his vision. He saw a hundred different types of cats, gnawing on dead carcasses, climbing trees in the African savannah. He saw blood and claws and sharp teeth, and the next thing he knew, he was leaning over the bed, vomiting into a bucket.

"It's okay...breathe," Rylee's voice soothed him, one hand holding the bucket, while the other rubbed circles along his spine.

Drew flushed in disgust and embarrassment. He'd never been sick in front of a boyfriend. He didn't want Rylee seeing him this way. He pushed his hand out, hoping to push him away, but the message must have read differently to Rylee, who grabbed his hand and held on tight. He wanted to push the hand away and shout he hated him, but instead, he held his hand tightly and cried as he was sick a second time.

"Shh," Rylee whispered, placing a kiss on the nape of his neck. "Everything is going to be okay. I love you, and I'm going to take care of you," he continued in a soothing voice. He wanted to listen to Rylee's voice and trust it, but his insides screamed. "I love Drew the man, Drew the cat...no matter what you are, I love you."

He wiped his mouth with the back of his hand, unable to believe Rylee would say those words. Not that *anyone* would say them, no, that Rylee would say them. And now?

A tissue appeared in his line of sight and he took it gratefully, wiping his mouth and brushing it against the back of his hand. It was stupid and humiliating, but he knew Rylee was telling the truth. He did love him, human and whatever the fuck kind of cat he was included. Nothing was going to scare him away.

When hands appeared on his chest and gently pulled him back from leaning over the end of the bed, he let them guide him. He closed his eyes to the feel of Rylee's strong chest pressed against his back, to nimble fingers brushing his pectoral muscles. It was soothing and appreciated. The touch gradually moved to the bottom of his shirt, then those warm hands slipped beneath it and worked their way up his chest.

Drew let out a sigh of contentment. It was good to have Rylee's hands on him.

*

After his mini freak-out, Drew felt better. He apologised to the boys, but they waved it off as normal. He wasn't sure the word had meaning anymore.

"Okay, now it's over, how do we find out what kind of cat I am?" he asked, trying to remain calm and think logically.

"Are you sure you want to deal with this now?" Lorcan asked with sympathetic eyes. "It's still early into your transformation, and I'm sure this is a lot to take in. You and Rylee should have a few days alone together, to talk and for the news to sink in," he suggested, full of reasonable logic he would normally applaud.

"We don't have time to wait, Lorcan. I appreciate you trying to put me first, but we're already down four days and have ten more to go. Then my hot-shot brother will barge into this house with a team of cops to search for the evidence I didn't bother to send him," he warned, eyeing them to impart the importance of the information and see it sink in.

"Do you realise how it looks to an outsider? Cat jokes, animal prints all over the place, murals of the Serengeti." He pointed to the one on Rylee's wall as an example and huffed. "I mean, for fuck's sake, you have a dungeon! My first instinct was to think underground BDSM club, but my brother has had a stick up his ass since birth, and he's never going to let his mind go there."

He ignored the chuckles from Keon, who found everything either hilarious or downright comment-worthy with a slice of sarcasm. Drew glared and reminded them of the danger. "You're fucked if they find Rylee's USB, which I found on my first search, because it's full of photos...which contain wild fucking cats!" Rylee placed a hand on the curve of his spine and began to rub.

"Baby, I think they get the point," he soothed, as though it had any bearing on what he'd said.

"Do they? Because I'm not sure anyone understands how hard my brother is going to be on you when he gets here. He's out for a promotion and the more people he takes down—innocent or not—the better he looks to his superiors," he confessed, truly believing they needed to know this, to prepare for the inevitable trouble Sheffield would bring to their home. "You can bet your ass if he thinks there are wild cats here, he'll have camera crews following every move they make. Even if we do manage to pull one over on him and convince him you guys are innocent, your faces will be out there, all over the media and any Tom, Dick, and Fuckbutt with a hunter grudge will know *exactly* where to find you."

Keon snorted. "So much for it being over," he muttered, wiggling an eyebrow at Lorcan, who rolled his eyes.

"Fuckbutt?" Delaware repeated, with arched eyebrows.

"Drew—" Lorcan began, until Rylee cut him off.

"Let him vent."

It was the last straw. "Vent?" Drew was hurt by the accusation. "Do you think I'm overreacting?" he wondered, stunned to think Rylee was ignorant enough not to see the forecast of what was to come. It seemed obvious.

"I think you're hard-wired to your emotions right now and can't think straight. I also think your hatred for your brother is making him into a supernova evil genius," Rylee replied, sighing as if Drew had become an over-reactive burden. "We're safe here, Drew. We always have been, and we always will be," he claimed, with such surety it drove Drew mad.

Getting to his feet, he looked around at them in shock. If they could be this obtuse about something important, they didn't have any right to his help. "That's the most ridiculous, selfish, egoist shit I've ever heard. And I dated Aniel!" he reminded him, practically screaming the words because it hurt to see his concerns being ignored.

"Yeah, as did I." Rylee looked unimpressed, and if any look could represent a bored yawn, it was the disinterest in his eyes.

"That's not exactly something to gloat about."

Rylee glared. "No? You can do it, but I can't? Does it make you jealous?" he asked, relaxing to fold his arms over his chest as though he didn't care.

"Jealous?" Drew experienced his first thought as a cat. Because no matter how smart or gorgeous he was, he wanted to claw Rylee's eyes out of their sockets and feed them to him. "Look here you piece of jungle shit, if you—"

His body was weak and tingly, his vision blurred by unexpected tears. His heart grew cold and vacant, like he'd already lost the warmth of Rylee from his life. Without Rylee, he had nothing. No one. How could he live without his soul mate?

Soul mate? Was that what the dumb tiger was? It would explain why it hurt to think about not being with him. To think he might want Aniel back, knowing what the bastard had done.

A cry escaped his lips which he couldn't bear to hear. It was high pitched and foreign to his ears. Drew didn't care what was happening. He was alone...truly alone...for the first time in a long time. He embraced all he had left—his cat.

With acceptance, the tingling turned into a sharp prickling beneath his skin. His vision became sharper and more pronounced, with slight coloured auras surrounding everything. When he witnessed the fur pushing through his pores, he fell to the floor.

Keening sounds fell from his mouth, but he had no involvement in making them. With no time to consider what was happening he was on four paws. The fur on his legs, when he looked, was golden and brown with black stripes and spots. Turning to look around the room, he caught his reflection in the mirror and almost freaked out again. His ears were long and pointed with little hairy tufts at the end.

He was a lynx.

His hands were paws and his vision distorted. He reached out his front paw, keening as he attempted to take his first unsteady step.

"There you go, baby." Rylee's soothing voice startled him into chirping a cry of surprise. A big hand landed on his head and caressed his fur, brushing his ears back and rubbing them gently. "It's okay. I had to push you. Extreme emotion is the best way to get there and you, gorgeous, are a hotbed of anger underneath the sweetness. I thought your brother or your dad, who was next on my list, could have been the trigger. It's sweet jealousy got you there, first," he claimed, keeping his voice low and caring.

Confused, Drew turned his lynx head and found most of the room spun. His legs wobbled, incapable of keeping him upright. Rylee got on his knees beside him and caught his body, drawing him to his chest.

"It's okay to be confused. Come here and lie with me." His capable hands helped Drew find the right movements to get him to lie down, curled on his side against Rylee's knees. "Guys, I think you're right. He needs time to calm down. He's got worked up trying to save us, and he's forgotten he can't do jack shit without getting his cat under control first."

"Well, I can always be the bait, if he can't get it in time," Keon offered, standing from his perch on Drew's old bed to shove his hands into his jean pockets.

By instinct, Drew growled and bared his teeth.

"Okay, it was a suggestion. Geez, you cats are crazy," he muttered, chuckling at his joke as he followed the others out of the room.

Lorcan offered a wave and a thumbs up, while Delaware smiled in a subdued way. They shut the door behind them and, despite it not being what his human had wanted, Drew was relieved they had left. Now, it was him and Rylee, and there was something about the fact his lynx loved. The same way he could feel the waves of love for Rylee's inner tiger seeping through his blood like it belonged there.

"I know, baby." Rylee kissed the top of his furry head. "I let you freak out, and I'm sorry. You needed to see the change will happen when you lose control. It's how it works the first few times, when you stop thinking and let your cat decide what's for the best," he explained, maintaining the soft, calm attitude which had infuriated Drew in the first place. "If you trust him, he'll lead you right."

Lifting his head, Drew couldn't quite figure out how to communicate with Rylee as a wild cat. He butted against his chest and thrilled when Rylee laughed.

"I love you too, baby," he whispered, saying the *L*-word without the amount of time together he would normally need to justify it. With Rylee, though, he didn't think *time* mattered. Emotion trumped time again and again.

Drew wanted to say something, but his cat was too busy enjoying the feeling of Rylee's soft jumper against his fur. When Rylee whispered one more truth, he decided to shove propriety and words to hell. Feeling was much better.

"You are the most beautiful lynx I've ever seen."

Chapter Twenty-Two

Drew woke in his cat body, curled into Rylee's arms. Blinking, he tried to get his mind to focus and realise it was more real now he was a physical lynx in body and partially in mind.

He lay his head on his hands—paws. Everything looked different but was still the same in many ways. When he looked at Rylee, there was a faint flicker of light which confused him. Drew leaned in and gave his mate a sniff—a mortifying thought to his human brain—and relaxed, at peace with the man he had fallen in love with.

His tiger.

Rolling onto his back, he delighted in the instinctive movement Rylee made, wrapping an arm around his lynx waist and shuffling in close behind him. Screw it, they lay on the floor, but he wouldn't want to be anywhere else.

Lowering his head, Drew gave Rylee's hand a lick with his coarse tongue and settled to sleep.

It didn't feel like much time had passed. He opened his eyes again to a sound from the doorway. Keon walked in with a blanket, offering a silent wave as he approached to lay the blanket over them.

"I love you like a brother, Drew. Please know I say this with kindness," he began, tucking the blanket around him with gentle hands. "Your lynx is beautiful, but I don't want to see you naked. Every time you change, your clothes are shredded and there's no repairing them. I stopped by earlier and threw out the scraps. In a few minutes, you'll change and you'll be butt naked."

Drew would have squinted at his friend to find out why it mattered, since he was with Rylee alone in their room, but he wasn't sure how it would look on a lynx' face.

Keon reached out and rubbed his ear, eliciting a rumbling purr which took him by surprise. His friend chuckled quietly. "It's about four o'clock. You have an hour to wake Rylee and grab a quick shag then you'll be expected to come down for dinner. The boys got you more food from the truck and they want to know how your first conscious change was," he explained, rising to his feet and leaving the room again.

It was nice Keon had come to take care of him. He didn't doubt Rylee would have done this had he been awake, but Drew knew the sense of letting him sleep. He'd been through the emotional wringer, finding out it was Aniel, the once-love-of-his-life who did this and the bastard was cheating on his sister with any human he came across. Knowing Aniel was in the human world and turning unsuspecting humans into cats. With how deeply Rylee was involved in protecting those who escaped Vihaan, he wouldn't want more hybrids wandering the human world unchecked.

Because they had to face facts, no one knew how long Aniel had been in the human world turning whatever human he came across with a single scratch. No one knew how many hybrid cats remained out there, mostly human but able to bring out their cat in a way true Vihaan's couldn't.

It was an utter disaster.

Of anyone, Rylee had earned the right to sleep and forget about those worries for a while.

Behind him, Rylee hummed and his breath huffed against Drew's sensitive tipped ears. "Turn round, baby. It's going to happen soon. Hold onto me," he murmured, still sounding half asleep.

He wasn't going to refuse the advice though. It was strange to roll onto his front and crawl towards Rylee in his lynx body. He couldn't roll over without kicking his boyfriend with four unwieldy limbs he didn't have full control over yet. Once he was tucked into Rylee's chest, he lay curled into a ball and waited for the change to take place.

A pain in his stomach hit first, forcing him to curl tighter. His cat yowled a cry of pain and received a soft shush from Rylee. A hand pressed against his back, holding him close and offering comfort. As another stab of pain shot through his legs, he growled a low burring noise as his cheeks puffed and he struggled to stay calm.

"It's okay," Rylee soothed, pressing Drew to his chest.

It didn't feel okay, but there was no arguing with the intense inner strength he could feel within his boyfriend, somehow reaching out to his lynx to let it know he was right.

Although it didn't hurt as much as it had when he became a cat, it was a small mercy. His insides stretched beyond their capability. At least once it was over, he felt better. Only, cold. And shaking.

Rylee seemed to know without being told, because he pulled the blanket tight around his shoulders and rubbed his hands over every inch in an attempt to heat him up. "You'll be fine. You need to eat more to fuel a change. Your body is going into shock because it's not used to the transition and you're not used to preparing yourself for it yet. Once you learn to eat what you can to fuel a shift, you won't suffer as much. Even the pain should go away," he said, hugging him tight and offering much more than the comfort of his words.

Drew never wanted to leave this cocoon of warm flesh and hard muscle.

"You've done well, baby," he continued, keeping his voice calm and low. "You accepted this easier than I ever hoped you could."

"It was...easy," he confessed, his teeth chattering as his entire body chilled like it had been plunged into an Arctic sea. "I saw...the signs...and it made...sense," he admitted, needing Rylee to know it would never have been an issue between them, even if Drew hadn't been marked for his own transformation.

Rylee kissed his forehead, his warm breath brushing his cheek as he sighed. "I can't believe you were meant for me. I never imagined I'd find someone who accepted me for who I am. Both now and who I was," he whispered, sounding sad. Drew wanted to cheer him up, but he didn't know how. "I can't let you go back to Aniel, baby. I don't want you anywhere near him. Not after what he did to you," he objected.

"I have another idea," Rylee confessed, kissing his cheek and rubbing his jaw along Drew's forehead. "If you tell Sheffield Aniel is framing us from a distance, but you've found evidence of his involvement at his house, he would have to investigate, right? Tell him you'll take Aniel out of his house, to a public place where you'll be safe, and give your brother time to get his team together," he explained, sounding hopeful despite the problems Drew could already see with the plan.

"While they're getting ready to pounce on Aniel the minute he gets back from meeting you, we'll plant the evidence at his place. Sheffield arrives to find it, he's arrested and it's over." With another rub of a soft cheek against his forehead, Rylee kissed his temple and continued. "You're right you have to be the one to draw Aniel in. He marked you, and it would look strange if you didn't confront him. It doesn't mean I'll let you put yourself at risk again."

Drew didn't see how they had a choice. Rylee had blinders where Aniel was concerned and had issues with the idea of either of them being alone with Aniel in a place not guarded by a hundred armed men. But that wasn't life and it wasn't possible to hide from Aniel's evil forever. A part of Drew knew he needed it. He needed to confront the bastard about what he'd done—the rape, the abuse, and turning him against his will.

He needed closure, and hiding wasn't going to give him that.

*

Deciding to take Keon at his word, Drew ignored further conversation and lifted his head to kiss Rylee's lips. As he'd hoped, Rylee was distracted by the soft caress of their lips and the slight push of one body against another.

He had successfully become a lynx. He had accepted his fate and, hopefully, changing would be a lot simpler and easier on his body from now on. Right now, it wasn't the cat inside Rylee he wanted to soothe, it was the fragile human heart within.

"Take me to bed," he whispered, needing a softer surface beneath him, not connected to his change, to distract him.

Luckily, Rylee was the strong, silent type and he didn't question Drew's request. He pushed onto his knees, grabbed Drew by his skinny waist, hoisted him onto his knees and lifted him to sit on the edge of the bed.

Without wasting time, he kissed his knee and began a tantalising trail up the inside of his thigh. Drew cupped his hand around Rylee's neck, loving the attention, and sighed when Rylee swallowed his bare cock whole. Which hadn't been what he was going for, but he definitely wouldn't refuse. Maybe he'd enjoy it later. Right now, he had something else in mind and it was much sweeter.

Winding his fingers into Rylee's hair, Drew ducked and kissed his cheek. "Kiss me?" he asked, knowing he needed to be clear about what he wanted. He wasn't the pull hair kind of guy when he was thinking clearly and he didn't want this to be something rushed and frantic.

As soon as Rylee dragged his lips slowly over the length of his cock and popped off, he lifted his head to offer the kiss Drew had requested. He couldn't help but hum in approval, leaning into the kiss and basking in the completely normal, familiar act which had nothing to do with animals or cats or Aniel. This was all them.

His fingertips danced across Rylee's cheekbones, revelling in the feel of soft skin against his. When Rylee broke the kiss and stood, while maintaining eye contact, Drew watched and waited. Rylee's T-shirt came off first, lifted to reveal toned stomach muscles, then bulging biceps as he lifted it over his head. As Rylee tossed it aside and lowered his hands to his jeans, Drew slid back to lie down and waited for his lover to join him.

This would be the first time they'd made love after the truth came out, the first time they'd done more than snuggle and share a brief kiss or two since this whole chaos started. What was sad was it was only the third time they'd had sex. Ever. He couldn't let this time together fly by. He needed to make it last and enjoy it to the fullest. Drew refused to take his eyes off Rylee as he knelt on the bed and climbed on to straddle his thighs.

"How do you know you love me?" Drew asked, unable to stifle the need.

Rylee lowered his weight comfortably over Drew's body. "Remember what I said about the red spark we saw?" he asked, leaning down to nibble his earlobe. "As the one with Vihaan blood, if I'd been the one to see it, it would mean we were destined for each other."

"But we both saw it," Drew recalled, sighing as those hot lips moved to lightly suck his neck.

Rylee hummed and swirled his tongue over his pulse, offering a light nip his cat instincts preened at. "There's a legend," he mentioned, drifting kisses up Drew's jawline and towards his mouth, "claiming if a Vihaan sees the flash, the mating is dictated by the Fates, not their hearts. But if a human can see the flash of light—marked or not—then..." He paused and kissed Drew's lips, lingering over the taste of his bottom lip and probing his tongue between them.

The moment Drew opened his mouth and caught the teasing tongue with his own, a rumble emanated from between them. Rylee chose that moment to break the kiss with a grin.

"Hear it?" he asked, lifting his right hand to brush the thumb across Drew's bottom lip. "It's the only proof we need, if we hadn't already known about your sight. Both of us seeing the flash means our cats chose each other. Our scents, our hearts, our essence...everything from your human blood and my Vihaan soul chose us for each other," he confessed, dipping to nudge their noses. "For me, it means more than any fated match."

Drew matched the Eskimo kiss and locked his fingers at the back of Rylee's head. "I agree. I knew you were special the moment I met you. I'd been scared for too long. Afraid to be alone with a man I didn't know, and afraid to trust they wouldn't hurt me. I was scared of opening up to a new boyfriend or lover in case they turned out like Aniel. Now, I'm with you, I can't imagine how I lived each day without hiding under my bed." Tilting his head, he brushed Rylee's lips with his own. "Thank you, Rylee. Thank you for wanting me and bringing me into your world," he whispered, marvelling at this unexpected turn of events. Being here with Rylee was where he belonged.

With one *almost* kiss, Rylee stole his heart, right here in this room. Right now, being here in this moment and making love couldn't have meant more to Drew.

Tipping his head, he pecked at Rylee's lips and whispered, "Make love to me. Show us we're yours. Both of us belong to both of you." Because that was how it would be from now on. Drew could feel it. They weren't two people anymore. They had become two cats who had chosen their mates and two people who had fallen in love. By acknowledging and accepting all four of them and their individual needs they would make this relationship work.

"Anything you want, baby."

Chapter Twenty-Three

Rylee couldn't put into words how it felt to have Drew with him. He'd never thought they could be anything to each other, when he first saw the spark and experienced nothing but grief because he thought it wasn't reciprocated. He didn't want a fated mate, he wanted something real. What he saw in those movies he'd watched since becoming human, what he read about in the gay romance novels a friend had introduced him to. He wanted the fairy tale.

Inexplicably, he had it. And he barely knew how to express his joy.

Drew was looking at him like he had found out magic existed—hungry, excited, but scared. Mixed in with a healthy dose of reality, recognising what this moment was and how much it meant. Because this was the start of everything they could have with each other. The start of a future spent together, if they could get Sheffield off their backs and distract him with something else. Right now, he wanted to give Drew everything he could see in his eyes. The love, hope and wonder. He wanted to put it into every touch and every move they made.

He started by touching his fingertips to Drew's collarbone and letting them wander. Always to a ghostly touch as they caressed the prominent bones of his collarbone, his jawline and cheekbones, to his forehead and through his hair to return to his chest. Caressing and exploring, as they drew invisible patterns over his abdomen and across his hip bones. Always drifting lower, one minute brushing over his hardening cock, then his balls and the tight hole he now knew well.

Drew sighed and his entire body tensed as he grasped the pillow beneath his head. Rylee could imagine the intensity of the anticipation and the fluttering sensations overwhelming Drew's body. No one had ever taken the time to explore him this way, in the same way he'd never explored anyone else with this intensity. Maybe one day, when this mess was over, he'd ask Drew to give him a night like this. To show him how it could feel.

Drew moaned, with a burr of total, complete pleasure. Rylee knew the moan intimately and it made him smile.

When those eyelids opened and he saw those gorgeous blue eyes again, his smile grew into a grin. He loved those eyes, endlessly expressive and beautiful. Their beauty grew when Drew smiled and he found his heart thudding frantically. He was full of love for this strange, accepting man. Sometimes it was too much to bear. He was beautiful and perfect and spectacular.

Drew rose to kiss Rylee's Adam's apple, lightly scraping his teeth over the sensitive skin. Rylee moaned in delight, tilted his head and caught Drew's open mouth in a sloppy kiss. Trading tongues as he lowered his body to the bed and returned his hand between Drew's legs.

Unable to wait any longer, he used his right hand to lightly caress Drew's tight hole and the left to grab the bottle of lube from the bedside table drawer. It was hard to function when Drew nibbled on his bottom lip and lifted his right leg to hook over his hip, raising his left to rest his calf on Rylee's shoulder.

He couldn't help but turn and kiss the bare skin. Drew had pretty much pinned him in place, but he'd never complain about the view. He flipped the lid of the bottle one-handed and dribbled a trail of lube onto Drew's half-hard dick.

"Why did you bottom for me?" Drew asked, somehow able to breathe steadily as Rylee used his right hand to spread the lube to his tight ass and loosen him up for what was to follow.

"What do you mean?"

"Well, I didn't think you'd switch," he admitted quietly.

Rylee couldn't help but laugh as he pushed his finger inside to a soft purr of approval. "I'm not a switch. It's part of the Mating. We have to share ourselves with each other, exchanging bodily fluids and submitting to each other," he explained, teasing him with a deeper touch.

Drew butted his head into the pillow. He was breathing heavily, despite the slow progress they'd made, but the way he moved his body, sucking in his stomach, pushing his chest up and dipping his head, the view was captivating. He barely knew what to do first. A part of him screamed to fuck Drew through the mattress, while another said to drag this out as long as possible.

"I've missed you," Drew whispered.

Rylee found his blue eyes glazed over with pleasure and focused on him. He wasn't sure what it meant, when they'd never spent as much as a day apart since they met.

"I want to get to know you better," he continued, tilting his hips enough to make his point clear: *hurry up*. "I want to know your secrets...your dreams...about your life in Vihaan," he said, panting his way through the words while Rylee offered liquid heat with every stroke of his finger. "I know you can't show me Vihaan, but I want to spend my...life with you...and spend our last day in Vihaan, together. You can go home and...you can show me...your home...your tiger."

The sentiment was beautiful and perfectly matched the decision he'd already made. If he knew he was living his last day or hour or minutes, he wanted to go home and die in Vihaan, despite how much it had limited his life and future. Rylee wanted to die a tiger the same way he'd been born one. To spend one last day with his tiger.

"I promise." He ducked to kiss Drew, sealing the vow with one of his own.

*

Once they had made love, showered, and ventured downstairs to join the other brothers for dinner, Rylee was pleased to see Drew had taken his advice to heart. He piled enough food on his plate even he'd have trouble finishing it. Drew took pleasure in every bite.

Selly cleared his throat to interrupt the silence and spoke with a grin. "I have good news."

"Oh yeah?" Keon perked immediately, which wasn't a surprise since nothing excited him more than gossip.

Selly nodded and quickly grabbed his can of Irn Bru, downed a decent drink and took a breath to steel himself. "I have a boyfriend," he admitted, looking ready to burst with joy.

A round of congratulations followed, and Rylee smiled. It had been about a year and a half since Selly told his parents he didn't feel like a woman on the inside. He was a man and always had been. When his family kicked him out, disowned him, and had him banished from Vihaan, Rylee had been the first person to see him in days.

Selly had wandered the human world, lost and confused from travelling through, disorientated by the change. He remembered the halfway house on his third day, *after* being victimised by name-calling, an attempted attack thwarted by an old man, and a whole heap of self-blame and shame.

It had taken weeks to get Selly back to his usual bright self, to get him to talk. Rylee had immediately applied to have him undergo transgender reassignment under the care of Doctor Robell. It was going to take a few years to get him where he wanted to be, but at least here Selly was able to live as the man he was and be known as a man.

To hear he'd actually opened up to someone enough to venture into a relationship warmed Rylee's heart. "I'm proud of you," Rylee admitted, reaching across the table to grasp his hand.

Selly blushed as he returned the grip momentarily, extracting his hand to return to his meal. "It's nothing huge. We've had the same classes for a while and, when he heard me saying to one of my lecturers I was a few months from leaving, he confessed he was running out of time to ask me out," he confessed, his blush growing darker.

Beside him, Drew sighed happily and shook his head. "He's awfully romantic," he said, the words turning Selly beetroot. "Is he a bad boy, a geek, or your regular old Joe?" Drew asked, curious enough to ask the questions, knowing how private Selly was, no one else would dare to.

To Rylee's surprise, he supplied the answers eagerly.

"His name is Brandy. He's actually from Vihaan too," he explained, biting his bottom lip. "When he asked where I came from, I told him it was a village called Vihaan and he knew right away. He sat there, shocked, and asked me if I was from *Gheva Tarlou, Pequij*—the city where our most humanoid creatures live—or if I came from *E'Boolou*."

"I take it that's another village?" Drew guessed, reminding Rylee of how much he didn't know about Vihaan. He would have to teach him, but he was also smart enough to know it had to wait. They had to settle this Sheffield dilemma first.

Selly nodded and provided the answer without hesitation. "Yes, it's where our half-humans live. Like Keon," he said, nodding to their friend across the table.

Keon's mouth was full of burger, but he nodded his confirmation.

"Huh." Drew shrugged it off and grinned at Selly. "What did Brandy say?"

"I told him I was from *Gheva Tarlou* and he said he was from *E'Boolou*. He's a wolf like Keon. Perhaps even part of his pack, once upon a time," Selly revealed, clearly excited about the revelation. "We've been going on little dates ever since, and, this morning, he asked me if I wanted to be his boyfriend," he admitted, flushing brightly.

"Like I said...a romantic," Drew claimed, sounding as pleased as Rylee was.

If there was anything Selly needed in a boyfriend, it was someone kind and romantic. Someone who accepted him for who he was and didn't look down on him. Someone he didn't have to keep secrets from.

Gesturing with his fork, Drew opened his big mouth and put his foot in it. "Is he understanding about this gender reassignment stuff?" he asked, about to receive a hard kick from Rylee for phrasing it indelicately and a serious talking to for bringing it up. "Because, if he's going to be a dick, I'll kick his ass. My friend Beck has been through the wringer trying to remind everyone he was never Rebecca; he played the part he'd been put in for those years. If you need backup, give me a shout."

Selly's mouth dropped open and, if the table had frozen when he opened his mouth to ask the damned impertinent question, it became a silent glacier drifting through the sea after his little speech.

Rylee could have kissed him.

Seemingly unaware of what was occurring around him, thanks to being too busy shovelling food into his mouth, Drew kept going. "Luckily, I had the perfect guy for Beck. He was a big deal at the local drag club—had the voice of an angel! I introduced them, they hit it off and poof! A year down the line they got engaged, and Beck had stalled his meds to try to conceive a kid naturally," he explained, sounding proud. It left Rylee speechless.

"He...he did?" Selly asked, with a faint frown.

"Sure." Drew smiled at Selly as he shoved another forkful into his mouth and chewed. Once he swallowed, he said, "He'd been on the hormone pills for about six months. When they agreed they wanted to at least try for kids, with Beck providing the world's most convenient incubator, they figured it was worth a shot. It took about eight months and help from IVF, but they did it. He's due in about three months."

Selly blinked so hard Rylee was worried he would hurt himself, and then he sagged in his seat and held a hand to his forehead. "I didn't know," he muttered, dropping his hand and rising from the table. "Sorry, I have to call Brandy. When I told him about the reassignment, he was great, but he asked if I didn't want kids like it was an option. I...I didn't know it was possible. I didn't want to give him the wrong idea and...I said no. I have to—"

Stopping suddenly, he left the room at a run, looking more excited than when he'd admitted to having a boyfriend.

Drew hummed and kept eating, while the rest of the table tried to recover from the shock of the conversation.

"You know," Martim said, gesturing with his cutlery as he looked around the table, "I think that's the most he's ever said at one time," he noticed, with more than a hint of confusion in his voice.

An unexpected chuckle escaped Drew, as he swallowed another bite and looked around at them. "Beck was the same. He was shy and reserved as Rebecca. Once he became Beck and he knew who were his friends and who were dicks, he opened up. It was like watching a butterfly emerge from a cocoon. It was incredible," he claimed, shaking his head with a fond smile. He stopped eating long enough to take a drink, then went to work on his plate.

When a scream of excitement erupted from outside the room, Rylee wasn't the only one who flinched and started to rise from the table.

Beside him, Drew patted his arm and said, "Sit down, tiger. Brandy's glad Selly changed his mind and is willing to keep the kid door open a little longer. He seems nice. And supportive, which is exactly what Selly needs."

The fact he could hear their conversation was disturbing, but normal for someone newly transitioned. His senses would be heightened, which would explain the exceptional amount of food he was shovelling into his body.Rylee returned to his seat and looked to Lorcan for an explanation of what was happening, despite his friend trying his hardest not to smile. He guessed Lorcan had a point. Who knew Drew and Selly would bond, out of nowhere, because this Brandy guy had come along and found the guts to ask Selly on a date?

It was—and he hated to think it—like fate.

Chapter Twenty-Four

Three Days later

They had run out of time and Drew was running out of patience.

"Again," Keon ordered, sitting on the bench in the garden, sipping from a cool bottle of Coke.

Groaning, Drew closed his eyes and attempted to reach out to his cat. He couldn't speak to him, since it seemed his cat was completely normal, because he wasn't capable of talking, but the purrs and growls were enough for him to understand. Right now, he was one pissed off kitty.

But this was necessary. He focused and repeated his mantra. *Bring out the cat. Bring out the cat. I am a lynx. I am a lynx, and it should be easy.* Yeah, right. It was frustrating, exhausting and not going well.

Squeezing his hands into fists, he took a deep breath and released it slowly, recalling what Rylee had said. Forcing his cat out would make him angry. He had to invite him, coax and bargain with him. Unlike everyone from Vihaan, his cat wasn't a natural part of his psyche or his body. He was a virus forced into Drew's bloodstream and his cat would feel he didn't belong, like he was never meant to be part of this team they'd become.

Drew's job was to convince his lynx it didn't matter.

Step one: name him. The most obvious choice was Felix, after the Latin name *Felis lynx*, but it sounded like a dog's name. He could also choose from Linnaeus, from the guy who named the species, or Kerr, after the guy who named the genus.

Yeah, he had spent far too much time on Google researching lynxes.

Kerr, it is, he decided. It sounded like a noise his lynx would make, was short, sweet and to the point. And not embarrassing to shout in a park.

Come on, kitty Kerr. We weren't born with each other, but we share a mind and body now, and we have to make this work. We're stuck together for life and…isn't it kind of cool we're more like Rylee? Because you know we both love him, right?

It was the sole tactic he could think of. He felt it every day. The more time he spent with Rylee, most of it outside of bed and training him for his future, the more he felt his cat burring with happiness and needing to be closer. He'd woken once or twice, rubbing his face along Rylee's chest and face, which had been mortifying until Rylee started cackling with laughter. Now, every time Rylee touched his hair or face, his lynx made rumbling noises of pleasure.

He couldn't go out in public unless he had Kerr under control. A slight shift offered relief, and something said his lynx was soothed by his reminder they did this for Rylee. Because he was right, they may not have been born to share their life, but being part cat made them more like Rylee and gave him a little bit of home. It was worth the pain and frustration, the sleepless nights and the damned infuriating lessons.

"You can do this, Drew. You have to accept you and your cat are one person. You're one mind, one body,"

Keon called out, the biggest source of guidance he could ask for. Of everyone in the house, Keon was the one who could still change into his animal. The other half-animals, or *Foame* as the Vihaans referred to them, had left to start their own life once Rylee had helped them rediscover control. They didn't need the makeshift pack the house had become for those banished or trapped in a human body.

The *Foame* had complete freedom in this world. Something Rylee didn't have.

Now, it was Drew's turn.

He contemplated what Keon had said. He and his cat were one mind. If it was true, then his wishes were his cat's wishes and Kerr's resistance was his resistance.

Like a lightbulb going off in his brain, Drew knew what the problem was. He didn't *want* to get his cat under control because it meant going ahead with the plan to frame Aniel and, deep down, he knew it couldn't work. Framing him was well and good, but his plan of getting close to Aniel again and having Keon there as backup didn't sit well with his conscience.

He knew what Aniel was like, how violent and manipulative he could be. Drew couldn't put his new family in his sights, to frame him for something which might not stick. They didn't know where Aniel had been, when, or what he was doing, if he had witnesses. What if their plan to frame him backfired and he had an amazing, bulletproof alibi?

No, their plan was bound to fail.

Rylee's compromise of getting him out of his apartment to meet Drew in a crowded place would never work either. There was no way in hell Aniel would agree to meet in public. He liked his home comforts and had trouble containing his temper. He'd want to be at home, where he could explode or let loose, where he had his favourite toys within reach. Where he was the biggest threat.

Drew needed to think of something else, but it didn't sit well that his help came in the form of an overprotective boyfriend, Lorcan's propriety and gentleness, and Keon's unpredictability. He couldn't drag them into anything to do with Aniel. What if he got his hands on one of them? What if he got his hands on Rylee again?

Drew's head burst with a full-blown headache. As he moaned and clutched his head in both hands, the worst case popped into his head. What if Aniel marked someone already from Vihaan? Would it kill them because they already had a cat inhabiting their mind and body and couldn't take another one? Or would it draw out their inner animal and make them a danger to themselves and everyone else they loved?

"Drew?"

He could hear the fear in Keon's voice, but there was nothing he could do.

Becoming his lynx was no longer a matter of proving to Aniel he'd transformed. It wasn't about utilising his cat if something with the plan went wrong. No, he needed Kerr, his sweet baby kitten, to come out to help save his family.

"You did it." Keon's voice was flat this time, lacking the excitement or wonder which should have been there. Drew lifted his head, to find his friend approaching with a faint frown. "It's impossible, Drew. I've never seen a newly turned transform without an excruciating amount of pain. How did you do it?"

Incapable of answering, Drew pushed onto four paws, realising he'd fallen to the ground with the shift, and butted his head against Keon's knee. He wanted to tell him he was the brother Drew had always wanted, he'd never let him get hurt, especially not by Aniel. He wanted to tell him he didn't know how he'd managed his shift, it was how Keon had said it would be—if he accepted he and his cat were one mind and body, it came naturally.

Once Keon had rubbed his ear, Drew backed away and took off running. The garden wasn't huge, and he had to do a few laps around the perimeter to give his legs a stretch, but it felt heavenly. To run and feel the air racing through his fur. Even fumbling in his steps and rolling to the grass was exciting and full of new sensations.

*

"You should have seen this one," Keon exclaimed over dinner at night, pointing his finger at Drew as he leaned on the table. "Running about the garden like a lunatic. Tripping over his feet and acting like a puppy."

Lorcan laughed as he brought a plate of steaming hot chicken to the table and let Rylee carve it. He took his seat kitty-corner to the house Captain and glanced to his right, where his boyfriend Mani sat gazing at him like a fool in love.

Drew loved seeing how happy everyone was here and it strengthened his resolve to protect them from the evil running through every fibre of Aniel's body.

"I wish I'd been there to see it," Rylee admitted, turning to flash Drew a sexy smile which promised it would have been fun.

"I would have turned, out there in the open, and you would have gone territorial because half of the house would have seen me naked," Drew argued, lifting the jug of lemonade to pour a drink.

In the background, Martim and a few of the other boys trickled in with plates loaded with food. He wasn't sure why they were laughing. "Too late. You walked through the upstairs hallway butt naked the night you first changed. Looked like you'd come right out the shower too." Martim winked at Drew.

"Well," he huffed, not sure how to argue when Rylee laughed, "I wasn't in my right mind at the time. It doesn't count."

"Sure, it does." Martim's boyfriend disagreed—was he Carlie? It was a unisex name, because Drew recalled he was one of the most successful transitions of the house, going through the surgery and hormone changes prior to meeting Martim. "You've got a cute butt and that always counts."

Martim burst into full-blown, belly-bursting laughter while Rylee scowled at the remark. Drew blushed. "Thank you. Yours is pretty cute too," he replied, since it was hard to ignore Carlie—he was sure it was Carlie—had a little bubble-butt which stood out no matter what he wore.

As he'd hoped, Martim's boyfriend blushed hard enough his freckles stood out. He burned brighter when Martim kissed his cheek and whispered something along the lines of his ass being both pretty *and* cute.

The hilarity died as the front door closed in the distance and they looked to see if Selly had returned from his date with Brandy or if it was one of the other brothers returning from a late class. Though meals in the house were a formal affair, there were no demands everyone must attend. There was plenty of food whether they showed up alone, with a group or didn't bother to show.

In this house, food never went to waste.

When Selly rounded the corner into the dining room holding the hand of a tall, dark and handsome piece of gorgeousness, Lorcan stood from the table.

"Hello," he said, too eagerly. "Welcome. Come join us, please." He gestured to the table where two people stood and grabbed spare chairs from the side of the room to place anywhere there was room.

"Hi." Selly blushed as he waved to the room at large and walked over still holding his boyfriend's hand to gesture to Drew. "This is Drew. He's new to the house, and he's recently gone through his first change. He's the one I was telling you about," he said, causing a flush to burn Drew's cheeks at the implication.

Offering a nod, and trying not to be too formal, he said, "You must be Brandy. I've heard a lot of good things about you. Will you be joining us for dinner?" He thought it polite to ask since the rest of the room had assumed it and the poor guy looked stunned by the attention.

"That would be great, thanks. I've always been a sucker for chicken," he claimed, laughing as he allowed Selly to guide him to their seats. After nodding to half the table in hello he turned to Drew. "I asked Selly if I could meet you, because it means a lot you were open with him. I know he's shy and he doesn't like to be the centre of attention, but it's good for him to admit he doesn't know everything, no matter how smart he is."

Drew had noticed. "I agree."

Brandy nodded with relief and began talking, slowly relaxing the tension in his shoulders. "I still remember what it was like when I was first banished. I'd never heard of this place, growing up in a sheltered family. I didn't know people in this world could help me," he confessed, his voice sounding troubled. As if things could have been different had he known about this house. "I was banished after I was caught kissing my best friend. He told everyone I forced him to, but he kissed me first. I was the one banished, though, because his family had power and influence within the community," he said, shaking his head in disgust.

Drew could feel the same emotion swirling around his veins. It didn't matter whether they were human or cat, both worlds were as prejudiced and politically driven as the other.

"I managed to find my way, after I came over. I hid in alleys and fields, fighting my instincts and trying to remember what had happened to me," he continued, sadness tainting his voice now. "After about three months of working crappy jobs as an illegal, I stumbled into an old man who knew about Vihaan. He said he could help me get new papers, legal documents and he'd teach me how to live as a human until I could build a real life for myself." When he shrugged, it was with a faint smile. "I wouldn't be here, with Selly, if it wasn't for him. He showed me what compassion was. I thought I knew everything I'd ever need to survive, but he taught me how to live."

Drew nodded along with Brandy, glad to have met him. "I know what you mean. No one here is an expert at how to be human, not even those who were human first. There will always be learning curves, and it's good to ask for help when it's needed," he admitted, relieved to hear Brandy seemed to have his head screwed on straight.

"Well, I was hoping you would talk to me about what it's like in the human world to...feel the way I do," Selly said, smiling at Brandy when his boyfriend poured him a drink. "I'm not sure where to find information other than what Doctor Robell gave me, and I have questions his leaflets don't answer," he confessed, as though it was a problem.

"No problem. Trust in me, young grasshopper, and we'll make sure Google answers your questions," Drew promised, with a wink.

He took a sip of lemonade and almost choked when Selly turned to Brandy and whispered, "Do you think Drew is okay? I'm a cat, not a grasshopper."

Chapter Twenty-Five

Hours later, Drew lay on the grass with Rylee watching the sunset create a patchwork of colour across the sky. It couldn't have looked more magical had it been painted by Michelangelo.

"Does the sky look like this in Vihaan?" he wondered aloud.

Rylee hummed and reached to catch his hand from where it rested on his stomach, winding their fingers together. "A little. The sky is normally this shade of red and gold, though. It's not the blue you have here. When it's about to storm it turns a dark royal blue in warning to get indoors."

"Do you have an "indoors"?"

"Yes." Rylee chuckled and squeezed his hand. "Most of us live in the habitat closer to what we are. The cats live in a jungle or savannah, the wolves live near caves and the foxes near burrows and grasslands. A whole host of creatures live in Vihaan, and we have our little areas carved out by scent," he continued, giving Drew enough information to imagine a half-human fox. The image which came to mind was a super-cute manga-style Kitsune. "The real problem with Vihaan weather is the rain seasons," he confessed with a thoughtful tone which said he should be thankful their two worlds were different.

Drew noticed the unexpected letter on the end. "Seasons?"

"Yeah, we have two full seasons of rain. The first is when you can see the clouds rolling in, drawing the water from the sea and it sprinkles throughout the jungle. It lasts a few weeks. The second lasts about two months, where it drops out of nowhere and it's not safe to go outside," Rylee recounted, a fondness in his voice which said he loved Vihaan, even if it didn't love him back.

"Rain in Vihaan is nothing like what you have here. The closest comparisons would be a normal day of rainfall here matching our lightest rain. A full rainstorm back home would be the equivalent of one of your human tsunami's," he explained, thoughtful enough to make a comparison he could follow and understand.

Drew couldn't stop from whispering, "Wow." The thought of Vihaan weather made him glad he'd never get the chance to visit the place. Though he didn't doubt the good days were as beautiful as the bad weather was vicious.

Beside him, Rylee lifted his hand to kiss his knuckles. "Yeah." He sighed when Drew shuffled over to rest his head on his strong chest. "We get one season of sunshine, one of autumn and four seasons of winter, where we transition from snowflake fall, snowfall, ice forming, and then ice breaking. Each one is as dangerous as the next, and winter is our hibernation period."

"It sounds...complicated."

"And a nuisance," Rylee agreed quietly. "I like having four seasons and being able to see the changes clearly. You humans get off lightly on the weather front."

Drew couldn't dispute it. Even the countries with the worst weather could hope it was a passing phase, stuck to the season. "Yeah, we're pretty lucky," he realised, unable to stop wondering if anyone in Vihaan had ever wanted an easier life. "When you were in Vihaan, living your cat life, did you ever wish you could be human, even for a day?"

"Sometimes." Rylee nodded, the movement ruffling his hair. "We knew about the human world, from the constant threat of being banished here. None of us ever knew what it was like. Most people who travelled here willingly didn't say anything good when they got back, probably from fear they'd be banished for the trouble, and those who were banished here could *never* come back.

"You see, the doorway between our worlds is about the will and safety of Vihaan. It's guarded on both sides by magic." He paused and sighed. "For Vihaan's like me, who were a pure animal on the other side, going back would mean the end of our human existence. Who we are here would cease to exist, and no one knows if we would turn back to our animal or if attempting to reverse the process could kill us," he explained, looking heartbroken by the thought. "Only the *Foame* can cross freely, used to trading between two bodies, two forms. Trading human goods with Vihaan's who are accepting enough to take them. They were the ones to share their stories, to tell us in whispers it could be safer here. We could be free here."

Drew couldn't imagine what it cost him to take in the strays from Vihaan, knowing they could go home when he would forever be banished.

He sensed the pain running through Rylee, as he remained silent. His lynx was hyper-aware of the prowling tiger beneath Rylee's calm façade. He wanted to do something, anything, to make his boyfriend feel better. What came out of his mouth was, "The human world was this huge mystery?" Attempting to get on track, and remove the reminder of his banishment.

With a huff of breath, Rylee replied, "Definitely. The more strained things became on Vihaan for those of us who were different, the more it seemed like a decent gamble. It couldn't be any worse here than it was there." The sorrow seeping into his voice made Drew burrow closer to his chest and wrap his arm across his waist. He wanted to keep Rylee as close as possible.

"I suppose it's true." What else was there to say? There could be rampant homophobia in parts of the human world, discrimination, violence and there were thousands more people like his dad in the world. But no one was banished from their own world to be sent somewhere which fundamentally changed their entire DNA sequence. Despite the hate and darkness, there were light spots where good people showed compassion and understanding, where havens like this house stood strong, waiting and willing to welcome anyone who needed somewhere safe to stay. He wished Vihaan had something similar. "I'm sorry you can't go back."

"I'm not. If I'd been able to, I would never have met you," Rylee claimed, lifting his hand to tip Drew's face up.

They shared a smile and, despite how happy his boyfriend looked, he couldn't help but make one last protest. "But you can't be your tiger again. You can feel him and sense him, but you can't ever run free again."

"It's worth it. I've spent twenty-five years as a tiger. After five years as a human, I could bear another twenty...or thirty," he promised, smiling until his entire body lit on fire. "It's like your experience, now. You've spent years being a human, and now you get the excitement of living as a lynx if you want to. The difference between us is you can suppress your cat if you want to. I can't suppress the human I've become."

Drew kissed him, because he couldn't resist. He needed Rylee to know how much he appreciated having him in his life, the guidance, the strong presence and the sure-fire knowledge he had someone in his corner, no matter what happened.

When he was rolled onto his back, he gave no protest, wrapping his arms around Rylee's waist and opening his mouth to deepen the kiss.

*

Guilt set in as Drew left the bed he'd become used to sharing with Rylee and snuck out of the bedroom with his mobile phone. He didn't want to get caught talking while in the bathroom. He tiptoed downstairs and didn't risk switching his phone on until he reached the kitchen.

With animal senses in the house, it would have been impossible to avoid being detected if his phone rang. Even harder to explain why he was sneaking through the house with his phone in the first place. At least if he sat in the kitchen with a drink and a snack in front of him, he could say he was playing games to pass the time, while feeding his newly increased transitional hunger.

Drew had the added worry of Brandy sleeping over in Selly's room, which normally wouldn't have mattered, but he had spent as much time in the human world as Rylee had. He wasn't like the others, with no concept or understanding of a lot of human things. Brandy was smart, definitely smart enough to rumble Drew's plan if he was caught.

He prepared his alibi in advance. He made a sandwich—which, in fairness, he probably *would* eat—poured a glass of milk and blasted it in the microwave for thirty seconds.

Once ready to say "see, that's all I was doing", if anyone caught him, Drew switched his phone on and immediately set it to silent. He opened his phone book and pressed Sheffield's mobile number to call him.

It rang for barely a second. "Detective Colley," he answered, sounding professional.

Drew stifled a laugh and replied, "This is secret agent Drew Colley checking in."

His brother sighed wearily. "I hope you're somewhere private where no one can hear you being ridiculous," he asked, bypassing any opportunity Drew had to reply. "Why are you calling this late?"

Taking a deep breath, he prepared his story and hoped to hell it worked out. "I think I've found something."

"Really?"

There was no reason for Sheffield to sound sceptical, but he ignored the immediate instinct to argue and answered the question. "Yeah. I need a few days to check it out. It's complicated," he explained, not sure how much detail to go into but knowing what his general plan was. As long as he could pull it off.

"The truth is never complicated, Drew. What did you find?" he asked, voice full of exasperation, as if he had a million better things to do.

"Sheffield, I'm sorry and I don't know how it happened, but...I think my ex-boyfriend is involved," he said, lying through his teeth. He *wasn't* sorry and he *knew* exactly how it had happened and, as there was *no* smuggling ring, Aniel *wasn't* involved. But he wasn't going to tell him.

"Your...what?"

Drew couldn't decide what made Sheffield trip over his words more, the fact he'd found something or one of his relationships was about to become the full focus of his case. Or the word "boyfriend" he couldn't bear to utter.

With a sigh, he elaborated and tried to drill it into Sheffield's thick, homophobic skull. "My ex. His name has appeared too many times for it to be a coincidence." On the other end, his brother swore like a trooper, making him want to laugh. It was a struggle to keep a straight face. "I know it potentially compromises everything, because you put me in here without knowing he could be connected. I'm asking for a few days," he continued, hoping to calm him. "I'd like to double-check the information I have, to run the lead and see if I can prove whether he's involved."

Sheffield groaned and there was a faint thump suggesting he'd banged his head against a hard surface. He hoped it hurt. "Fine. Do you know the guy well? I mean, were you serious?" he asked, still not using the all-important word.

"Semi," he replied, not sure how else to put it since he'd spent half the relationship too scared to leave Aniel and not knowing how to escape. "He...he wasn't the nicest person. It would be within his wheelhouse to be part of something like this. But my other problem isn't going to make you any happier," he hinted, hoping to ease him into the next bit.

With a drawn-out sigh, Sheffield muttered, "Spit it out."

"I don't think anyone here at the frat house has any idea what's going on," he said the words fast, knowing it wasn't what Sheffield wanted to hear. There was no way he could explain what was happening. He'd never believe there were two worlds with a connecting door which turned cats into humans and humans into cats. He'd have Drew locked up before he could say "kidding".

"How can they not know there are wild fucking cats on their property?"

"I'm not sure there are."

Silence reigned. Then the familiar dulcet tones of Sheffield's voice boomed down the line. "What are you talking about? We've got DNA samples and eyewitness accounts of wildcats seen or heard within the property. Are you trying to sabotage this for me, Drew?" he demanded, as if he'd ever risk it. He had taken this job for the money—a fact they both knew well—and he'd get the money *after* the case was closed.

"No. I want to make sure it's done right," he argued, trying to remain calm. "You know me. I'd never let an animal be hurt or put in one of those fucking circus shows where they're made to fight or where they're hurt for profit. You know this," he reminded him, adding enough of a bite to his voice to get the message across.

Sheffield sighed and it sounded calm, somehow. "You're right, I'm sorry. This is a huge case. This could make or break my career," he protested, as if it mattered.

Innocent lives were at stake. He couldn't imagine what it would do to any of the guys here if they were locked up for something they hadn't done. Their cats would go crazy locked in a prison cell.

"I know, which is why I'm asking you to give me a few more days," Drew reiterated. "I know this guy. I know how he thinks, how he operates and what he's likely to do if I confront him. I'm going to be smart. I'll double-check everything first, and, in the event he is involved, I'll make sure you and your guys can go in armed with the information you need."

"Okay. Are you sure you don't need backup if he was...violent before?"

Drew rolled his eyes at the way Sheffield couldn't say it out loud. But he wouldn't argue. He didn't much want to say the words either. "Thank you, but no. Like I said, it's complicated, but I'm sure I can handle him. If not...let's say I'll prepare for every eventuality."

He hung up, not willing to hear Sheffield's remark or talk about Aniel any longer. Not when his brother dared showed the first sign of compassion Drew had seen in years.

A second later, his phone vibrated with a text message from Sheffield. *You have three days. If I don't hear from you by then, I'm arresting everyone at the frat house.*

Smiling, he couldn't help but type his reply. *Agreed.* He set his phone aside and lifted his sandwich. He had to steal the "evidence" he'd need to frame Aniel, phone the bastard to arrange a meeting and slip out of the house tomorrow night to put his plan into action.

And figure out how to say goodbye to his boyfriend and the family he'd found here, in case it went to shit.

Chapter Twenty-Six

The next day, Drew dedicated his entire day to Rylee. They spent a lazy morning in bed, paying detailed attention to every freckle, then ate brunch on the front lawn, watching the world go by.

When they were both free for a few hours in the afternoon, Drew followed Rylee along a trail in the local forest. He wasn't sure where they were going or why, but Rylee had brought one backpack and a cooler, saying they were staying to have dinner in the thick of the trees. He wasn't sure why the backpack was needed if he already had the cooler, but he kept quiet and promised to let it be a secret until they arrived at their destination.

In the centre of the wood, in a small clearing, Rylee stopped and turned. "Let your cat out," he said, with a smile that didn't stop growing.

At first, Drew thought he was hearing things, then he registered the truth of the words and goggled at his boyfriend for a full minute. "Here? Out in the open?" he asked, worried it was a bad idea.

"I paid the security guard to lock the access gates. If anyone wanders in, they don't have permission to be here and any sighting of you can be passed off as a drunk or hallucination," Rylee promised, a sparkle of hope in his eyes.

Drew looked around again and smelled the fresh, forest air. What he wouldn't give to run through a forest as his lynx and let Kerr out. He wanted to, but he was scared. He didn't know if he had the control not to hurt anyone, but he could also be reported as a wildcat escaped from somewhere. If anyone caught him he'd be in real trouble. It would reach Sheffield and convince him his original idea of an illegal wildcat smuggling ring was true.

It seemed Rylee had worked it out beforehand. He looked hopeful.

A pass was needed for the security gates into the forest, which Rylee had. If no one else had the pass, the gates wouldn't open. But they could be climbed. Drew's head told him Rylee was right, anyone reporting a lynx in the forest would be considered a nutcase and ignored. If he heard anyone nearby, he could transform at will. Yes, he'd be a guy wandering naked through the forest, but there were worse things to be.

"I don't know." His analytical brain imagined far too many possibilities for arrest or danger, which could be reported to Sheffield and ruin his plan.

Rylee caught his face in his hands. "I do. I promise I'll be right by your side. I have a blanket and spare clothes in my bag. If you hear someone coming, we can have you covered quickly," Rylee explained away Drew's fears.

"Fine, but you have to catch me." He bit his lip as he backed away a step, letting the transformation take over.

It hurt like a bitch, but he gritted his teeth through it and continued to crawl away from Rylee. It took a few minutes, and, once he was fully within his lynx body, he turned and took off running, smiling on the inside at the sound of Rylee's laughter as he attempted to catch up.

He never wanted to stop running. He ran as far as he could go without losing sight of Rylee, then turned and ran again. He calmed to a slow pace and ran alongside

Rylee, who ran at full speed. It was heavenly to let go and let both sides of his personality run free.

There was no way to make it better without Rylee's tiger by his side. That was a dream for another day, one far into the future when they were old and grey, embracing their last day on earth.

*

The day had passed quietly and without any issues, like Drew had experienced the calm before the storm. His human-self was more capable of bonding with Rylee now Kerr understood what was at risk. Kerr had to do his own bonding, through touching, sharing emotional intimacy and by being in the same space as his boyfriend.

Knowing that also explained why he was whiny and needy at the moment. His cat didn't like having his time with Rylee cut short or being interrupted by other people. Kerr wanted Rylee, alone, one hundred percent, seven days a week.

Over the day, Drew discovered he was getting better at differentiating his reaction to Rylee and Kerr's reaction. The purring was permanent and not a phase he was going through. The more he and his cat bonded with Rylee, the more often it happened. What eased the embarrassment was the fact every time he purred, Rylee smiled. He claimed every purr, burr, and sound of delight from Drew's cat spoke to his tiger on a primal level and made him feel wanted as a mate. Drew had no problem with that.

The more he and Rylee got to know each other the stronger his feelings became. He wasn't sure if there was a feeling beyond love, but if it existed, he experienced it. It was crazy and stupid, but he enjoyed it. It made him feel safe, because he knew Rylee would never leave him. If he could stick around long enough to teach him how to control his inner cat, to welcome him into a world he was never meant to know about, then he wasn't likely to run any time soon.

Despite his plans, Drew appreciated the way Rylee had taken care of him, treating him to a special day out, away from distractions, pressure, and the other brothers at the house. Kerr insisted Rylee was being a good soulmate by taking care of him and looking out for his emotional welfare.

It was still surreal if he was honest, but he'd trusted Rylee since they first met and there was no reason to freak out about something natural and…almost…fated. As if the entire reason he'd suffered Aniel as a boyfriend was for this moment to be possible, because it had been Aniel who set in motion the change which made him who he was right now.

While his boyfriend packed away the container for the food he'd brought for their picnic, Drew's phone chirped out a text message and his sneaky, underhanded plan fell into place.

"Sorry. I forgot to switch it off," he apologised, hating the lie, but knowing it was for the best. He grabbed his phone, deleted the text he'd scheduled to have sent and typed out a message for Aniel:

Need to talk. Can I come to your place? 2 am?

He didn't expect a refusal. Drew put his phone onto silence and pretended to be reading the imaginary text he'd received. When his phone buzzed in his hand, he wasn't surprised by the reply.

Yes. Come alone. Bring wine.

It wasn't a romantic date, but Drew decided against replying. He deleted both texts and switched his phone off. If Rylee had to check his phone between now and 2:00 a.m. he wouldn't see anything incriminating. He didn't have time for delays if he was going to see his plan into fruition.

The hard part was done. He had photocopied the evidence which didn't incriminate anyone within the frat house and written a note asking Sheffield to keep the photos private, to not let them go to court if he could avoid it, because it would be breaking the privacy of the "victims" by revealing their faces to the public.

Amongst the "evidence" and the note to his brother, Drew had included a one-page letter to the boys of the house, a two-page letter for Keon and Selly, while it took nearly six pages to say everything he could think to put into words for Rylee. An explanation, his feelings, how it had changed his world to be made into a half-human and meet the boyfriend who had somehow healed his shattered heart.

Cuddling into Rylee's warmth as they lay on the blanket after a long run, with Drew wearing the change of T-shirt and joggers Rylee had thoughtfully provided, Drew couldn't imagine a better day. "Thank you. I haven't done anything to deserve a whole day spent on me, but I appreciate it."

"You do a million things every single day to deserve a whole day for you. I haven't had the chance to show you, what with you being sick and preparing for this plan with your brother," Rylee disagreed. "You've had a lot to deal with. You needed to focus on you for a while."

Drew shrugged off the praise, letting his hand slip around the back of Rylee's head and card through the short strands of hair at the base of his skull. When Rylee's fingers found their way into *his* hair, he felt Kerr rolling over and basking in the touch. He wasn't sure why, but his human and cat both loved the comfort of having strong fingers in his hair.

Right now, he marvelled that Rylee would want to touch him. He had endured a hell of a lot and never complained. He'd been caught in his own mental chaos and it wasn't fair. They were a partnership, a duo: friends, boyfriends, and lovers. They should look out for each other.

Leaning on his elbow, he smiled at Rylee and kissed him, deciding to make the most of this moment alone together.

Responding with a slow, gentle kiss which had his toes curling in his shoes, Rylee pushed up and moved to lie over him. He broke the kiss and grinned. "You're beautiful when you get lost in the moment. It's like the rest of the world fails to exist anymore," he noticed.

Drew couldn't help but blush at the compliment. "You make me feel like we're alone in the universe, you and me. I'm all you see, hear and want. Like I'm your first and sole priority in life," he confessed, keeping his voice to a low whisper.

Rylee kissed him quickly, shifting to straddle his thighs. As Rylee gazed at him with awe, running both hands over his chest, lifting them to caress his thumbs across Drew's cheek, he lay frozen, unable to say anything as he stared at this incredible man.

"I can't imagine my life without you," Drew said softly, afraid this could be his last chance to say goodbye before the world went to shit. "You've made me happy. It's as if I've been walking in a dream my whole life, waiting for you. I know we haven't been together long, but I know how I feel. You complete me." He let out a sigh of happiness. Drew stared as Rylee's lips curved into a smile. But he didn't want a smile, he wanted to be kissed. He opened his mouth and brushed a kiss over Rylee's lower lip to get his attention. He was finally kissed back, seconds had them tongue-tied and lost in the moment.

Rylee kissed him like they would never have another day together and, right now, was exactly how Drew felt. It was what he needed, to know they'd made the most of this time together before Aniel and reality crashed into their privacy. "I love you," Rylee whispered against his lips.

Unable to stop smiling, Drew hummed. "I love you." A slight buzzing sensation travelled through his limbs and he thought he sensed his cat taking pride in the feeling, but he wasn't sure. What he did know was Rylee had secured a partner for life. However long Drew's life lasted after tonight.

It had been an idyllic day, everything he could have hoped for and more. He had finally let his lynx out for a real run, he was with Rylee, they were entirely alone and they had the rest of the evening to bask in each other.

Drew knew it was real, but it was hard to believe. It had to be a dream. One he never wanted to wake from, knowing what lay on the other side.

Chapter Twenty-Seven

As great as it had been to spend the day with Rylee, Drew couldn't put off the inevitable any longer. Once they returned to the frat house at the end of the day, he played along with their normal routine of hanging out with the boys, going to bed and sleeping beside Rylee. Until his watch beeped in a reminder he had to go.

It was one o'clock and he was dog tired after the long day, but he had no choice. Slipping out of bed required careful planning, but once he was free of Rylee's draped arm, he grabbed his prepacked satchel and left the room. Knowing he needed to take extra care, Drew had a set of clothes to change into, the evidence he'd need and his mobile phone updated with a voice recording app to make sure Sheffield had Aniel's confession loud and clear. Using any of it, however, was on the "trial and error" side.

He crept along to the floor bathroom, changed into his clothes and left what he'd worn to bed in the laundry basket. He pulled out a thick manilla envelope from his bag and crossed to Selly's room.

Knocking lightly, he was pleased when Selly opened the door immediately. "You're definitely doing this?" he asked, leaning against the door frame while worrying at his bottom lip.

"I'm sorry. It's important," he apologised, holding out the envelope.

Selly accepted it and held it in both hands while Brandy appeared behind him.

"Good luck, Drew. You're doing the right thing," he said, offering the encouragement he needed to see this through. He offered them both a nod of gratitude. His nerves had been shot for hours, but Drew knew this was how it was meant to be done. He couldn't think of any other way to keep the people he'd come to care about safe. He backed away from the door and walked along the corridor, down the stairs, and out the frat house, making sure to lock the door behind him.

It was done. Selly had his "goodbye" pack, and if, by breakfast tomorrow morning, no one had seen or heard from Drew they would have the answers they needed in Selly's capable, trustworthy hands. Unlike Keon, who would have opened it immediately, or Lorcan who would have made him answer twenty questions first, Drew knew Selly trusted him enough not to dig too deeply and not to go against his request. He would have Brandy there, to share the secret with, but would have no inclination to break his vow and open the envelope too soon. It would cause panic if he did.

Once he was out in the open, Drew grabbed his mobile from his pocket and called Sheffield. He knew there would be no opportunity once he was within Aniel's house to get a phone call or text message to his brother, and, with Aniel's house on the opposite side of town to the police station, it would take Sheffield time to get a team together and get permission to come to the rescue.

Doing it now was better.

It rang and rang, as he'd expected. The call was finally redirected from Sheffield's office number to the front desk. After the polite woman asked what the reason for his call was, he had to take a breath to find the right words.

"This is Drew Colley. I'm working as a consultant for my brother, Detective Sheffield Colley," he began, waiting for her recognition of his "position". "Can you please inform him I'm heading to the suspect's house as agreed? I have a recording device and will make sure to get his permission to record his words to ensure it can be used as evidence. I also have the confirmation he is the suspect we've been looking for. In five minutes, I will no longer be reachable by phone or text."

"Thank you, Mister Colley. I have your information. Do you require backup?" the woman asked in a pleasant but slightly nervous tone.

"No, thank you. Sheffield and I have this timed carefully, but—" He stalled, because he knew what Aniel was like. "—if anything does go wrong...if this goes completely sideways...he'll find a letter of explanation at the fraternity house, along with a detailed list of the evidence I've found. Please ask him to be considerate when breaking the news to them. I...they're my friends and...my boyfriend will take it hard," he admitted, not sure he should be saying this to her, but not knowing what else to do.

He'd thrown this whole plan together at the last minute, and he and Sheffield didn't have anything "timed carefully". But he knew his brother would be itching to make a move the minute this woman passed on his information. He could only hope for the best.

"I understand, Mister Colley. God be with you," the woman replied calmly.

Drew grumbled a thanks and hung up. It wasn't God he needed on his side tonight, it was luck.

*

"Would you like a drink?" Aniel asked, with the patented smirk Drew had once found sexy as hell.

Drew shook his head and looked around the living room as he stepped inside. It hadn't changed much, it was still like a scene out of *The Picture of Dorian Gray*. Dark, gothic and lacking colour, it was the epitome of everything Aniel was. Lonely, darkness hiding in plain sight, and with a hint of evil lurking in the shadows.

He perched on one of the single armchairs, refusing to choose the sofa where Aniel would take the liberty of sitting too close. As it was, the pale, dark-haired boy who looked like him when he was a few years younger, seemed to hold Aniel's undivided attention for the moment.

The leather collar around his neck and the fact he wore nothing but a pair of leather chaps were disturbing reminders of his brief time as Aniel's boyfriend. When he was naïve enough to want to do anything to please Aniel, when he didn't question the "role-playing" and thought it was fun. He never saw it coming when it turned too serious and violent for his stomach to handle.

Sitting here, it returned to Drew in stark crystal clarity. Of course, it hadn't been the way at the time. He hadn't realised before he left how much Aniel loved to control his "boyfriends". It started with a shared joint on their first date, then became a regular nightly smoke. With the copious amount of alcohol they consumed at clubs and parties, Drew soon lost track of their partying habits.

It was coming down from the high which frightened him. Drew had never been one for taking drugs. He'd accepted a sniff or two from the poppers Aniel pushed on him during parties, along with the regular joints, but he'd been convinced they were harmless. Everyone else used them.

Those first few weeks after leaving, Aniel had shown him the truth. The doctors had told him the rest. He'd been systematically drugged with small doses, building a habit over time, and required a serious detox at a rehab clinic for six months afterwards. Drew remembered the shakes, the fear, the anger consuming him after learning what had been done. He'd never told anyone, not even Rylee, because he'd been responsible for trusting a shit like Aniel in the first place when the warning signs were there. But he'd thought he was in love and love had trumped common sense.

It hadn't helped him recover. It hadn't helped him understand why a compliant boyfriend needed to be slipped uppers and downers whenever Aniel thought it appropriate.

Understanding the bastard was the furthest from his mind. It had been too long ago to press charges and he hadn't wanted the attention at the time. Watching the poor guy sitting where he'd once been, Drew knew he'd made a mistake. He'd been selfish, thinking about his reputation, what it would do to his family, what his family would do. He hadn't thought about who took his place.

This guy looked barely twenty, with dark rings around his eyes. Either Aniel had used him harder than he'd used Drew, or the guy had been with him for a while. He couldn't have been his first replacement. There was no way this boy had survived two years with the hard-living Aniel forced on their young bodies.

"Andrew! Pay attention!"

Drew snapped out of his thoughts and turned to where Aniel stood over him, meeting his gaze instinctively, remembering the rules about paying attention, maintaining eye contact, and always doing as he'd been told.

"Are you jealous?" Aniel smirked at Drew, then turned to the boy. "Pet, why don't we take you to your room and leave Andrew and I to talk in private?" he suggested, already walking towards the poor boy.

Drew tried to offer a look of reassurance and comfort, as if it would help, but he was caught by the terror in the boy's eyes. He didn't know what to do. He *had* to get him out of here.

As soon as Aniel left the room, Drew grabbed his phone and dialled Sheffield's mobile. He vaguely heard his brother answering groggily on the other end, but he ignored it. He didn't have a lot of time. "I'm at Aniel's house. He's got a young boy here who is terrified. He's a prisoner and he's doped to the high heavens," he confessed, a familiar fear choking him, "like I was." He hung up and returned the phone to its recording function, not wanting to be caught.

With the job done, he pulled the photographs from his bag and raced over to the bookcase against the right-hand wall. He had to scan the shelves for the one he wanted, since Aniel had rearranged them since he'd last been here.

Finding the classic story *Pygmalion*, which was about trying to alter a person's fundamental being, Drew slipped the photographs into the pages randomly. Littering in pages he'd printed from Rylee's journal with a few modifications he'd added. Mostly they talked about how Rylee had trouble controlling his cat and keeping it at bay. The modifications focused on Aniel's superiority complex, believing he should be able to do whatever he wanted, along with a few stories—told in Aniel's POV which it had killed him to write—about the time Drew had spent with him. He made sure to point out he hadn't fallen for the "cat" fantasy and it was the reason Aniel got rid of him.

With them printed and tucked into the book, he hoped the cops would find them and believe they were put there by Aniel. For now, he returned to his seat and took deep breaths.

He hadn't realised how quickly it would come back and how terrifying it was to be in Aniel's clutches again. Drew knew he was strong. He'd survived everything the sadistic bastard had done, but coming here was like reliving it with the added panic of *"What have you done?"* One truth was evident...he'd been an idiot. He'd willingly walked into the lion's—or tiger's—den, not knowing how the hell he was going to escape.

If he ever would.

For certain—once Aniel got back from caging his current boy-toy, Drew was in trouble. He'd caught the glimmer of excitement in his dark eyes, he'd smelled the arousal the minute Aniel opened the door, and his cat was scrambling beneath the surface, desperate to be let loose and claw Aniel to pieces.

None of it would happen. If he didn't keep his wits about him, he would endure a few hours of reliving the past in horrifying detail, unable to trust anything else, again. Worse, if he couldn't fight Aniel he had no right going back to Rylee. He couldn't let this start again and go back to Rylee to justify what he'd done tonight. Saving Aniel's current victim and getting the bastard locked up would be worth it, but he doubted "I *had* to" would be enough for Rylee.

If he ever got to see him again.

Drew had been such a disappointment he'd been thrown out of his own life, his home and their relationship two years ago. He'd been a failure. And Aniel didn't tolerate failure.

Maybe hoping Rylee could never forgive him was for the best? Because the more he thought about it, the more Drew realised he wasn't leaving this house alive.

Chapter Twenty-Eight

Drew choked on his tears as he realised the awful truth. He tried to fight them off, to hold them back or wipe them away, but he wasn't quick enough. Wasn't strong enough.

Aniel walked into the room yammering on about how "his boy" was secure for the night and stopped short once he saw the state Drew was in. "What is this?" he asked, his voice returning to the low, gritty register which spelled trouble.

"I'm sorry," he whispered, knowing he had to fall into old habits or ruin everything. "I'm sorry I failed you. I'm sorry you had to replace me. I didn't realise how much it would hurt to see you with someone else," he lied, knowing there was no other reason he could give without suffering for it.

With a hum sounding suspicious and intrigued, Aniel took a seat on the sofa, laying his arms over the back of it while crossing one leg over the other. "Why don't you come sit over here and tell me how much you've missed me?" he suggested, a teasing lilt hoping for more than "tell me".

Drew shook his head without realising he was doing it. "I couldn't bear to disappoint you again," he lied, closing his eyes to prevent vomiting at the thought of saying the words. Reaching into his bag, he held out his mobile and laid it beside him on the arm of the chair, the recorder already running to capture his agreement.

"Would you mind if I recorded you? I need to know what I did to fail you, and I need to keep it with me, to remind me why I don't deserve you."

Aniel arched an eyebrow. "I will give you this, because I know how comforting you will find it to have my voice with you for always," he said, either mocking him for what he considered a weak attempt to capture a piece of him for sentimental reasons or rejoicing in the thought Drew needed him again.

"I need to ask you to explain what I did, but could you tell me why you drugged me?" he asked, needing a few answers which would also count against Aniel whenever he was arrested. This was his best chance. "After we...separated...my doctors said I'd become dependent on uppers and downers."

A chuff of laughter seeped out of Aniel. He sniffed and shook his head. "You were always curious, Andrew. Always seeking answers when there were none," he claimed, while surveying the room. "You were insolent when you came to me. Untrained, unreliable, and lacking discipline. Yet you were resistant to every lesson I ever taught you, every piece of guidance I gave, you fought back and refused to believe what I told you was true. I had to take certain...steps...to ensure your compliance. Once I did, you were ready to be retrained and retaught."

He made it sound simple, logical. Once upon a time, Drew would have bought it with ease. Now, he wanted nothing more than to scratch his eyes out. "Does your new boy need the same encouragement I did?" he asked, needing to know whether this other prisoner would be resistant to an escape.

"He's well beyond that stage now," Aniel remarked, waving the matter off without a single trace of concern. "I found him in a BDSM club, fresh-faced and innocent, having never ventured into a relationship of this kind. He needed no other encouragement to behave than a little attention. He learned quickly what the consequences for misbehaving were and what rewards he would receive for being good."

Drew remembered them too. A scratch, a bite or a whipping for good behaviour wasn't his idea of a reward. Being beaten to a bloody pulp until he lost a tooth or two wasn't exactly what he called a consequence for misbehaving either. The consequences could be worse, like his last night in this room. He'd rather not think about it.

Zoning into the conversation, he listened to Aniel recount the various torture methods he used on his new boy, smirking whenever he mentioned something he'd loved doing to Drew. He didn't stop him from rambling on, because it counted as evidence against him. As long as he made it out of here alive.

When Aniel stopped, Drew shifted in his seat and waited for the inevitable. "We both know why you're here, Andrew. Why don't we discuss it openly?"

"No. I don't want to talk about what you did to me, yet," he refused, unwilling to put on tape that Aniel was a tiger from another world currently trapped within a human body. And he'd scratched Drew, implanting Vihaan blood into his system and turning him into a fucking lynx.

He liked his sanity and his freedom, thanks.

Typically, Aniel shrugged it off, as he did with anything he didn't want to punish at the moment. He liked to save his punishments for one allocated point of the day where it hurt more to have them compound on one other.

"Did you mark him?" Drew didn't see the harm in asking. He could twist them to mean something else later if he had to. He wanted Aniel's honest reaction.

"Naturally," he replied, flashing the damned annoying smile again as he rose from the sofa and crossed to stand in front of Drew's chair, forcing him to look up or stare at his crotch. "I turn my favourite boys. Those who please me...who desire me...even the ones I must release but want to return to me when they are more capable of obeying me," he explained, sending chills down his spine as Drew realised what he meant.

"You always intended for me to come back?" he whispered, turning away because he couldn't bear it any longer. He didn't want to be here, didn't want to look at Aniel, remember he existed, and he didn't want to accept he'd been manipulated even after Aniel set him free.

A touch on the underside of his chin tipped his head, too strong for Drew to resist. He knew what happened when he did; a backhand which stung for hours, a bite to make him scream in pain or a fist to the mouth. Explaining to *another* new dentist why he kept having "accidents" and losing teeth.

When Drew thought about it, as their eyes met and Aniel licked his lips while staring at him, he had more crowns, bridges and repairs done to his teeth than a rugby player. "Why did you hurt me?" he asked, unable to swallow the one question he'd always wanted to ask. "I loved you. I did everything you ever asked of me. It was never good enough and you always punished me for things I didn't do. Half the time I hadn't done anything wrong, but you hurt me anyway," he recalled, hating the tears falling unchecked.

Leaning down, Aniel used his rough tongue—cat-like, leaving him wondering why he'd never noticed—to lick away his tears. It didn't matter if Drew flinched and tried to turn away, Aniel held him in place and took what he wanted. Like he always did.

"You were always sensitive, Andrew," he muttered against his cheek. "You had to learn love is a fallacy. You never obeyed me from love. You obeyed because you were eager to please me. You had to learn all that would ever please me would be hurting you." One more lick made him shiver with fear, as those lips moved to his ear and whispered,

"I'll take you back, Andrew. I'll show you how it feels to push beyond your boundaries, to travel beyond pain and become more than my companion. I'll make you my accomplice. I'll make you in the image of myself, train you and teach you how to be like me. First, you must learn your place...and your cat must recognise when to bow to a more powerful predator."

The first punch was to his gut, forcing Drew to curl in. A hand pushed against his shoulder, tossing him to the floor of the living room where he lay for the next hour.

*

Aniel was true to his word. He taught Drew a whole new level of pain than he'd ever experienced. Or, maybe the reason it hurt was because his mind wasn't dulled by constant numbing drugs.

He bore it with all the strength he could muster. In the back of his mind, when the kicks and the brutal slam of a boot against his bones was too much to bear, he repeated his mantra, *Sheffield will come.* He'd been a shitty brother, but he was a great detective and would do his job. He would be here with a whole team of cops, to rescue Drew from his own stupidity.

Kerr prowled within his mind, restless and itching to be released to fight back, but Drew couldn't allow it. He didn't need the cops barging in to find a wild lynx in the house with no sign of the Andrew Colley they expected. It had been the plan, once. Until he realised they would put him in a cage and lock him away from any hope of escape. Or worse, an idiotic, trigger-happy cop would shoot him for being a threat.

He forced his lynx to wait, letting it offer mental strength and resilience until he could get out of here. Which, unfortunately, meant leaving as a man.

As Aniel ranted and raved above him, stomping on his wrist, Drew was distracted from the pain of the break by movement at the living room doorway. Aniel had left the door open when he got back from seeing "his boy" to his room, probably to let the sound travel and make him jealous. Or as a warning they could be replaced.

Seeing the pale face and Kerr telling him this boy was "family", shocked Drew more than he could fathom at the moment. His mind had shut down to protect itself, but he managed to understand family meant Vihaan. Which meant Aniel had forced this sweet boy through a transformation and kept him.

When the innocent kid curled his hand around the door frame and made to take a step, Drew shook his head and let a growl of warning escape.

"Yes," Aniel said, too stupid to notice his "pet" freezing behind him with a confused frown. "Tell me to stop. When you stop begging for mercy, you'll be ready to stand by my side as you once did. This time, you'll be there as my equal and we'll bring the world of Vihaan to a new era!"

Drew almost rolled his eyes at the posturing but ignored him in an attempt to communicate with the boy at the door. He set his jaw tight and locked eyes with him, trying to tell him it was okay, they'd be safe soon. They *had* to let Aniel rant and rave for this to work.

The boy didn't seem to understand, but he hovered in the doorway, eyes wide with fear. If it was fear for Drew, he needn't have worried. He was encased in pain, each new kick and the stomps trying to break his body and mind barely registered. They were a scratch on an already numb wound.

It was his mind that couldn't take much more. Reliving flashes of his old life. One he hadn't walked away from soon enough. One which had left bone-deep scars he had tried and failed to run from.

When Aniel's boot collided with his head, Drew moaned and watched his world darken around the edges. He wasn't ready to pass out yet. Not when Aniel could turn his temper on his "pet" as soon as he was done with Drew.

But there was nothing he could do. Scrambling to remain conscious made him feel dizzy. Too soon, the world took on a blood-red hue, and a bang was followed by a scream. Comprehension was lost in a haze of reality as he blacked out into peaceful, pain-free oblivion.

Chapter Twenty-Nine

It was bright when Drew opened his eyes again. Bright and blinding.

Blinking didn't change that. He shut his eyes, wondering why the pain had stopped. Had Aniel drugged him to make the worst of it go away? God, he hoped not. It was hard enough to go through the treatment once, he wasn't sure he could do it again.

"Drew?"

He frowned at the familiar voice, wondering why it wasn't Aniel's and why he wasn't being called Andrew. He hated the name Andrew. Always had. When Aniel started using it, it seemed poetic. The man he hated most in the world calling him by the name he hated.

"Drew!"

The shout did it. He snapped his eyes open and blinked at the image of Sheffield slowly coming into focus. "What are you doing here?" he asked, frowning at his brother as he tried to put the pieces together.

"We arrived at the house as you passed out," Sheffield explained, shaking his head in exasperation, while drawing a metallic stool closer to perch on. "As soon as we burst in a kid came screaming for help, saying you were being murdered. We got you out of there and had you checked by the paramedics. You have a broken wrist, a bruised collarbone and a whole shit-ton of battered ribs. You're lucky to be alive."

The condescending, lecturing tone was familiar and Drew couldn't help but smile. Lucky to be alive? He was lucky every bone in his body wasn't shattered to pieces. "Love you too, brother."

"I'm serious," Sheffield snapped, then groaned and lowered his voice. "We arrested Aniel for attempted murder, domestic abuse and the unlawful imprisonment of a minor. The kid you say was your replacement is seventeen," he revealed, surprising Drew since he'd been sure Aniel was smarter. Unless the kid lied about his age at the BDSM club to get through the door?

Closing his eyes again, he decided to contemplate the problem later. Then he realised how uncomfortable he was. "Where am I?" he wondered, blinking his eyes open again to look around him.

Hospital was not the answer.

Turning to glare at Sheffield, he catalogued the dingy walls full of posters, the coffee/kitchenette area in the corner of the small room and the battered sofa against the far wall. "Am I in the staff room at your precinct?" he guessed, unable to keep the growl from his voice.

Sheffield rolled his eyes—the bastard—and folded his arms over his chest. "The paramedics wanted to force medicate you and were talking about putting you in with a shrink. I couldn't let them compromise the case. I need your statement. I can't let any treatment fuck up your recollections. Be grateful I allowed them to give you painkillers," he grumbled.

Knowing what he meant and why he worried, since his brother was smart enough to have tracked his medical records and claim them pertinent to his case, Drew began to talk. There was no reason not to, now. He explained about his history with Aniel, to give him an idea of what the poor kid had been through, and hoped it would be enough.

Once Sheffield assured him Aniel had found the boy a few months ago and he'd been compliant due to his submissive nature, he changed direction.

"Aniel is…insane. That's the easiest way to put it. He believes he's an animal who came from another universe and he's trapped in a human body in this universe," Drew began, laying the groundwork for a nice cushy padded cell in a psych ward he hoped Aniel enjoyed prowling around in. "He believes his "boys" are his true mates and they have to pass tests to prove their worthiness. Because he's a "tiger"—the King of the jungle, in his mind—it gives him the right to treat us lesser humans any way he wants."

Sheffield hummed and continued writing as Drew talked. "It tallies with what the kid told us. Aniel's a tiger and he "turned" the kid," Sheffield explained, giving Drew exactly the information he'd expected to hear.

"Yeah, well, he uses a shit load of drugs, mostly in drinks or food—and you can check my medical records to prove he did it to me, and he's got a pattern of abuse—then he starts trying to brainwash us into believing we're cats too." Drew tentatively lifted his right hand, wincing at the copious amounts of gauze wrapped around it, to rub his right eye.

"Because of the drugs, his "boys" are convinced they're wild cats. I never believed it, which was why he got rid of me," he revealed, though it was far from the truth. "He always makes sure to scratch us badly, as if in proof of what we are. I've got the scars on my hip and shoulder. I'll testify to how they got there, if I have to," Drew admitted, not relishing the idea.

His brother nodded, his hand flying across the page of his notebook as he took the statement. "This kid we rescued. He says he's a bobcat. Aniel thought he deserved to be punished for not being good enough. You think he needs psychiatric treatment?" Sheffield asked, looking at Drew for the first time.

"No." God, it would be a disaster. "I promise, once he's off the drugs and he's safe again, he'll know the truth. Don't pressure him into talking to anyone, because the memories hurt like a bitch. It's bad enough living through it without having to go into detail over and over again," Drew confessed, realising what he was saying after the words were out.

He noticed Sheffield looked uncomfortable. Drew kept talking to cover the slip. "I think the kid would be best with me. I can take care of him, get him the right help, and he'll get to see it's possible to survive Aniel without ending up insane," Drew said, hoping it meant he could take the poor kid to the frat house and get him the help and support he needed to live the life of a cat.

"Sounds fine to me. The psychiatrist who examined him said his mind is too fucked from the drugs to testify. He doesn't know what is real and what isn't. He wouldn't be a reliable witness in court," Sheffield said the words like they were nothing. Like the kid hadn't been down the rabbit hole, torn to shreds and spat out again. "It's probably a good job he played along though. The doc looked at your notes from back then and said this kid barely has half of what you were on. He's probably not been with Aniel long or he played along well."

Drew didn't want to dig into the pit and try to make Sheffield see sense. He wanted to get out of here. "Did you find my bag?" he asked, realising the evidence he needed was inside.

"Yeah." Sheffield turned away and returned with an evidence bag with his satchel inside. "We'll go through it later. The Captain wanted to make sure you'd live long enough for us to use it, first," he remarked, smiling as though it was his attempt at a joke.

Knowing they'd have used it whether he lived or died wasn't an argument worth starting. "Aniel left me alone, to put the kid in another room. That's when I called you and snooped. I found photographs and journal pages tucked into a book. *Pygmalion,* I think. I was talking to you at the time and I don't know if he removed any after I passed out, but they were in there."

His brother nodded, either in agreement they'd been there or in understanding of what he was saying. "We have a forensic team sweeping the place now. We'll find it. There's a lot of hair coming back with animal DNA."

"I bet Aniel's found a drug to make it happen or he's surrounded himself with actual wild cats. I wouldn't be surprised if he tried to attach them to his own head," Drew rambled on, wondering if it was a step too far towards incredulous. It was the one part he hadn't reasoned away, but with how crazy Aniel was, maybe the cops would believe anything was possible? Unable to think of an alternative theory, Sheffield's phone rang in time to save the day, and his brother stepped away to answer it.

Drew's head throbbed and he badly wanted to curl up to sleep. He didn't know if it was an hour or two after he entered Aniel's house or if it was morning already. He wanted to get out of here and he wanted to see Rylee.

"Thanks." Sheffield clicked his flip phone shut and returned to where Drew lay on what appeared to be a side counter. "That was my partner. He's at the house overseeing the evidence collection. Seems they found photographs labelled before, during and after, with wild cats in the picture. He's going to have them tested to see if there's any way they were photoshopped to fit his delusion or whether he hired out wild cats for a one-off photoshoot. It probably explains the hairs we found," he explained, sounding like he bought it and Drew wouldn't have to scramble for another explanation. "Explain what this has to do with the frat house you were sent to investigate."

Ah. He'd forgotten. Thinking quick, Drew decided on the shortest explanation, "Rylee, the house Captain, is Aniel's ex."

"Explain."

Drew sighed. He should have realised it wouldn't be enough. Not when he'd spent weeks—was it weeks or was it a few days? It was hard to remember—living at the frat house and claiming he'd found nothing. "Rylee was engaged to Aniel years ago," he said, since mating wouldn't have helped his case in this instance. "But Aniel refused to step out of his closet in a town where it wasn't accepted. He married Rylee's sister. Between then and now, I haven't got a fucking clue what happened." And he didn't. Whatever had gone on, it likely involved Aniel cheating on Rylee's sister or being banished from Vihaan for being a bastard. "Aniel's been furious with Rylee for trying to make him come out years ago, and he likely took it out on me and everyone after me, hoping to throw it in Rylee's face. A *look what you made me do*." At least, that was how it went in his head. Without any proof of what Aniel had been thinking—and did it matter what motivated a man who was both violent and fucking insane?—it was conjecture. "I think he planned this. He knew I was in town, he knew you were a cop, and he used it to get to me. He manipulated us, as petty revenge which would make me crazy, upset Rylee, and get me back in reach again. He...fuck, he can't let go."

Sheffield snorted and glanced up with a wry smile. "When we arrested him, he said we had no right to touch you. You were his 'property'. I'd say the crazy-ship sailed long ago," his brother agreed, for once.

"That's for damned sure." He winced as the pain started to seep through whatever painkillers he'd been given. Drew decided to cut this short. If Sheffield wanted anything else, he'd have to come to the frat house to get it. "The kid you rescued...can I talk to him? I want to make sure he's okay," Drew asked, not sure if it was allowed.

"He's giving his statement to another officer, but I can get you five minutes."

"Thanks."

An awkward silence followed until Sheffield closed his notebook. "When you were with Aniel...the first time...did this happen a lot?" he asked, gesturing to the state Drew was in.

Considering he'd had minimal medical attention, he was probably covered in bruises, cuts, blood or a combination of all three, with a bandage around his wrist to show for it. "Sometimes," he replied, not sure why it mattered. It was in the past, exactly where he hoped it would stay. "It could be worse, at times, or not as bad. It was good at first, the way it always is. They lure you into a false sense of security, thinking you're in love and are loved in return. Then the real monster comes out."

Wasn't that how it always worked in relationships? The devil made promises he or she couldn't keep, using them to gain their victim's trust and affection. When they finally revealed the truth, there was always something stopping them from leaving—nowhere else to go, no one who cared, a baby or a family member who was being used against them. There was always something. With Drew, it came down to a serious lack of self-worth and the master manipulations of a man who knew his weaknesses.

"Why didn't you say anything?" his brother asked, eyes downcast, actually appearing upset or conflicted. Maybe guilt over never caring to see what was right in front of him? Now he couldn't avoid it, he was being forced to see his own failings.

Drew raised an eyebrow at Sheffield, who watched him carefully. "Not for nothing, but you can't accept I'm gay unless it benefits you. Why the fuck would I come to you about an abusive boyfriend I was too terrified to speak out against?" he wondered, hoping he had an answer. He wanted to know why Sheffield thought he deserved anything. Why he'd been alone with the secret and couldn't turn to his family for support.

"I'll get you those five minutes," he muttered, in place of an answer.

"You do that."

Chapter Thirty

It took an hour for Drew to see Aniel's latest in a long line of victims. An hour where he'd been able to convince Sheffield never to use the photographs in court, because it would destroy the lives of those innocent victims who had managed to escape Aniel. For once, his brother agreed.

The boy looked his seventeen years and not one day over it, as Drew was led into a comfortable waiting room with two sofas and a coffee machine. His name was Denny.

When he heard the door shut behind Drew, he raised his head, eyes wide and hopeful. Drew held a finger to his lips and gestured to the cameras in the room. He hoped since they were both cats, talking in whispers would be fine, since they'd hear each other, but the camera wouldn't catch their words.

"I'm Drew," he said, sitting a comfortable distance from the guy. "I...I was Aniel's boyfriend two years ago, until he got rid of me," he explained, hoping to show Denny why he'd been at the house and they were the same.

Denny nodded. "He talked about you a lot. He wanted you to be the one who succeeded where the others had failed. For you to go through the transition and join him. He wanted to make more of us, to overrun the human world with half-animals," he whispered, rushing his words in panic.

"Yeah, I guessed as much," he confessed, remembering something along those lines in amongst his rampaging rambles. "I hear you're a bobcat."

"I'm sorry!" Denny gushed, eyes big and panicked. "He asked me to tell the truth and...I didn't know what to do. I could sense you were a cat, and the cop freaked out about the condition you were in, saying you were his brother. I thought he was one of us...I thought he knew," he admitted, worried he'd done wrong.

Shuffling closer, Drew lowered his voice. "You did well. Always tell the truth. I'm sorry to say, it also worked into the story I gave them," he said, and began explaining how this began. He ran through getting dragged into the case, entering the frat house, who they were and why they were there, and his own transition. As quietly and quickly, as vaguely, as possible.

"I've told them Aniel is insane, believes he's a cat and believed we were too. Don't worry, your story tallies with mine," he promised, trying to reassure him it would be over soon. Aniel would never deny his heritage; he never had, as far as Drew knew. He wouldn't start now. "When this is over, do you have somewhere to go?"

Denny shook his head and started crying. "I've been homeless since I was fifteen, when my parents died. I got tired of living on my own, you know? I wanted someone to take care of me," he confessed, sniffing back tears of shame.

Knowing better than to touch him, after what Aniel had done, Drew smiled. "You can come live with us? There are a lot of cats in the house who can't change because they were banished, but Keon and I are both half-animal. You wouldn't be alone, and you wouldn't have to keep it a secret. We could learn how to be half-animals together," he offered.

With another sniff, Denny nodded and crumbled into endless sobbing. Drew sat there, offering company and the occasional tissue, while he changed the subject to better things. Like the future. And what it was like to live a happy life well away from Aniel's influence.

*

"I'm going to fucking kill him!" Rylee curled his hands into fists as he paced the floor in the dining room.

"You may not have to," Keon grumbled as he read the letter of explanation Selly had handed over.

It was nearly eight in the morning, and they hadn't heard from Drew. When everyone began questioning why he wasn't in the house, and Rylee remembered how cool his side of the bed had been, Selly had stepped forwards with the envelope and confessed to the promise he'd made.

He didn't like that Keon could be right. By going to Aniel's house alone, Drew may not have survived. If he did live through it, he wouldn't come back the same man.

Rylee knew better than anyone how manipulative Aniel could be. He'd never experienced the violent, vindictive side Drew had, but now he knew it existed, he also knew Aniel had no morals and no limits. Not when it came to lashing out in anger and taking what he wanted, regardless of the force or violence required to get it.

The thought of Drew being alone with him sent chills up his spine.

Raking a hand through his hair, he contemplated the next logical move. Phone Sheffield? Phone the local hospital? Try Drew's mobile first? A jolt shot through him when the doorbell rang, interrupting the roll call of options.

Rylee marched out of the room and threw the door open, praying Drew would be on the other side. He was...and he wasn't. A man almost identical to Drew, but without the spark of curiosity and laughter in his eyes, stood in the doorway. Tall and imposing, dressed in a suit, a coldness in his eyes which would never be in Drew's. And two uniformed officers standing behind him.

His heart rate stuttered and words failed him. This was it. This was the moment he heard the news which would destroy him. Drew was dead.

"Rylee Brobak?" the man in the suit asked.

He couldn't move. Couldn't speak. His mind was as fractured as his broken heart.

"Um, excuse me." Lorcan pushed him aside and smiled at the man. "I'm sorry. Rylee's in shock at the moment. We've discovered Drew Colley is missing. My name is Lorcan. Would you be Drew's brother, Sheffield?" he asked, somehow keeping his wits about him when reality was staring them in the face.

Hadn't he realised these men had come to tell him Drew was dead?

"I would." The man offered a tight smile as Lorcan gave Rylee a shove to get him away from the door.

"Please, come in." He stepped back and held the door as Sheffield turned to the two men with him and said something to make them walk away. Once they left, he accepted Lorcan's invitation and stepped into the house. "Please have a seat. I'll tell the boys you're here," he said, giving Sheffield no time to speak, though his horror was evident, as Lorcan bustled out of the room.

He returned with half of the house trailing behind him, perching around the room or hovering as they waited for news.

It took time for Sheffield to adjust and for Rylee to make his way over to the sofa to sit beside Lorcan. "Is he dead?" he asked, unable to stop the words.

Sheffield deflated with the question and relaxed into his seat. "Not yet," he replied, with enough grit to suggest he would be the one committing fratricide. "He's lucky. I thought he'd be dead or have half a broken body to contend with, but he's strangely okay," he revealed, sounding a touch mystified. It could be his Vihaan blood working. It was stronger now, because he was still transitioning, and would have probably healed the worst wounds quickly, without leaving much damage. It was a small favour.

"He's alive?" Lorcan asked, with a frown demanding *where is he?*

"Yes," Sheffield replied quietly. "We got him medical attention, took his statement and we've got Aniel Jamoor in custody on attempted murder and the unlawful imprisonment of a minor, for a start. More may be added later, but I think he'll be locked in a psychiatric ward for criminals," he continued, reaching up to rub his eyes.

Slowly, he gave them a shortened version of what had happened during the night. How Drew had called Sheffield to say Aniel had another victim, they'd arrived as Drew passed out—what Sheffield thought had been his last breath, at the time—and the questioning and process of what happened after.

"I'm telling you this against the rules," Sheffield said, with a warning glance saying he would deny it if they admitted it to anyone. "Because though my brother doesn't tell me shit about his life, I know when I'm being lied to. When I asked if anything would compromise this case in court, he flat out told me "No". His eyes were screaming yes. I checked in with my surveillance crew," he revealed, turning to look Rylee in the eye.

"You're dating my brother," he said, not asking or confirming, but stating a fact. "He's in love with you, you know. I can always tell when he's fallen into the pit, and this time he's worse than ever. He told Jamoor's victim— a seventeen-year-old kid—he could come live here with you. With *all* of you. I thought he meant until the trial, which probably won't happen if Jamoor is criminally insane. I overheard them talking about how they can take classes together and train together, how Drew would always take care of him. How he'd take him to therapy and rehab."

Pride swelled in Rylee's chest as he listened to Sheffield. It didn't matter how much he disapproved of what Drew had done. It was the way Drew had stepped up and become a source of protection and safety for this teenager who needed them. If he spoke of them training together, it meant this boy had been scarred by Aniel and had undergone his transition or was about to.

He wished the stubborn brat was here so he could kiss him for it.

"Drew's going to need all the support he can get over the next few weeks. If this goes to trial, he's agreed to testify about his past relationship with Jamoor, to show the judge there's a pattern of behaviour," Sheffield went on, with a troubled frown. "He won't talk to me. You need to be there, because it's going to be hard. If Jamoor fights this, they'll use every dirty moment of their relationship to paint Drew in a bad light. Probably drag up those old tabloid photographs too. You'll need to present yourselves as character witnesses if you want to help him survive it."

"Agreed," Keon spoke first, and then Lorcan gave a nod.

In front of his eyes, Rylee saw the boys step up. Agreeing to support Drew. Offering to testify on Drew's behalf, to prove he was a good person.

With a nod, Sheffield got to his feet and stepped away from the sofa. He stopped after two steps and hesitated. "Drew's in the car. I asked him to let me speak to you first," he said, explaining why he hadn't brought Drew with him. "He's been through a traumatic event, and, though the doctors can't explain it considering his injuries, he doesn't have a concussion or anything to hold him back from healing. Maybe you could let him sleep for a day or two and not bombard him with questions."

Lorcan smiled as he stood, when Rylee should have been the one to do it, and crossed to where Sheffield stood. "Detective Colley, in this house, no one ever has to explain anything. We're a family, and when one of us is ready to talk, the rest of us will be ready to listen. For now, Drew will need a lot of rest, care, and quiet. We'll make sure he gets it."

Without seeming rude, where Rylee would have grabbed Sheffield by the arm and dragged him, Lorcan guided him to the door and saw him out with a polite goodbye.

With no memory of moving, Rylee found himself at the open door, staring at Drew as he bundled out of the cop car and limped two steps. The moment he lifted his head, tears came to Drew's eyes and he lifted his good hand to his mouth to fight them back. The boy beside him, wrapped in a blanket and wearing little, walked silently by his side.

He wanted to run to Drew, to sweep him off his feet and yell his relief to find he was in one piece. But his feet were frozen to the spot as he watched his boyfriend limp along the path, accepting a helping hand from the younger boy to climb the steps, while pressing a hand to his stomach.

Once they were on the doorstep, Rylee backed up and Drew took the one step left to get into the house.

The second the door was shut behind him, Drew shuffled over and tipped forwards, his forehead hitting Rylee's chest. "It's good to be home," he whispered.

Rylee closed his eyes and wrapped his arms around his strong, stupid, brave man and hoisted him off his feet. Drew held on tight, wrapped his legs around Rylee's waist, and erupted into heart-wrenching sobs.

Epilogue

Six Months Later

"Why did you do it?"

Drew snapped his attention away from where Denny's hand sat comfortably in the grasp of his first boyfriend since the whole Aniel incident. Thinking about how much effort and pain it had taken to get to this place; the therapy, the medical care, and the rehab counselling required to have Denny here, this happy, able to trust another man to be his boyfriend.

"Well, I knew no one would buy the whole wild cat story," he admitted, finally answering the boyfriend, Brence's, question.

He was a bobcat, too, like Denny. He was a friend of Brandy's and had found out about the frat house and its "safe house" reputation after joining Brandy for a family barbecue. Which meant any Vihaan in this world was welcome to gorge on the delicious Vihaan food truck they'd hired for the day.

"If we framed Aniel for running the illegal smuggling op, there would still be cops and regular people worrying about wild cats being on the loose. Which meant if they stumbled across one, there was going to be trouble," Drew explained, letting Brence in on the big secret of why he'd gone to Aniel's house alone. Despite having visited them for the last two weeks, since he first asked Denny out, this was the first time he'd ever asked to know the story of how they met.

"They bought the insanity story?" Brence wondered, sitting back to lift an arm around Denny's shoulders.

Drew nodded, grabbing another muffin from the tray on the table and digging in. "Definitely. They had a psychiatrist give him a mental eval and he told the truth. He's a tiger from Vihaan, which is another universe attached to ours by a door which can turn wild cats into humans."

Everyone laughed, because they knew how nuts it sounded. Nuts or not, it had saved them from Aniel's deluded plans and saved a whole host of innocent humans from being cursed with Vihaan blood against their will and abandoned to figure it out on their own.

In the first month after Aniel was arrested, *Foame* began appearing at the frat house. The newspapers had mentioned the house had become a "refuge for Aniel Jamoor's victims" after his arrest. Any human he'd forced to transition or any lost *Foame* and Vihaan who read about the case knew this was a place of safety for those with Vihaan blood.

Rylee took in as many as he could and, when it proved too difficult, Drew convinced him to branch out. With the money they received from Aniel's estate—restitution for the pain and emotional torture he and Denny had been through—they were able to buy the house next door, from the university, and use it as their extended safe house.

When Rylee applied to have it converted into a charitable organisation for victims of domestic abuse, the university had chipped in remodelling money and had a local TV gardening crew come in to make a "relaxing and therapeutic" space in the garden.

It was a nice place to hang out as a human and great for the cats to relax on a hot night, but they still went running in the park once a month. The *Foame* took the time to let their animals out, while the banished Vihaan natives had a picnic and lamented their inability to join them. They played baseball or rugby, anything involving running, in an attempt to show off the power in their human legs.

It was one more sign of acceptance which made them feel like family.

*

By the time Denny and Brence left for a movie date, Drew was tired. He'd had nightmares after the Aniel debacle, especially while they waited to hear if there would be a trial. Aniel was crazy in front of the evaluation team. The judge deemed him a danger, stating he should be locked away for a life sentence in a psychiatric mental facility for the criminally insane.

As long as he refused to lie about who he was he'd never be let out. It didn't stop the occasional panicked nightmare imagining what would happen if he did or if he escaped. Drew had gone back to therapy, both for his own sake and to show Denny it was worth the time and effort required to get anything out of it. Doctor Robell had studied psychiatry and was treating them both. Neither had to lie about being a *Foame* or about what they were going through.

"Hey."

Drew hummed as Rylee sat beside him on the new swing chair in the garden. "Hey yourself," he replied, opening his eyes to see his boyfriend watching him closely.

"You okay? I didn't expect Brence to question you," he admitted, sounding troubled. Which was adorable, but not necessary.

"It's okay. I can't pretend it never happened," he reminded Rylee, as Doctor Robell continued to tell him. His past would never go away, no matter how deeply he buried it. Like last time, trying to pretend it never existed would make it harder to face when something dragged the memories to the surface again. Maybe if he'd dealt with it the first time, he wouldn't have been vulnerable when facing Aniel six months ago. "I have to be able to talk about it, Rylee. As much as I wish I didn't, it's important. And you need to tell me how it affects you." It was something Rylee had trouble with. Drew had noticed Rylee went quiet whenever Aniel's name was mentioned, and he'd go for a run after he put Drew to sleep after a nightmare. He couldn't keep bottling it inside and refusing to let Drew see it hurt him.

He took a deep breath and challenged the problem head-on. "I know it hurts you I went alone, but you have to tell me. You have to trust you can tell me anything and it won't break me," he promised, laying his head on Rylee's arm to show him nothing could tear them apart. "I know you don't understand, but did you ever ask yourself *why* I had to go alone?"

"No. Just you being stubborn and pigheaded," Rylee complained with a whole load of fondness he couldn't hide.

Smiling at the victory, he corrected Rylee's assumption. "I did it because I love you. I see how important you are. You're the glue who brings these lost Vihaan's together. You, Rylee. You're needed here, and if I'd have let you come with me, Aniel would never have said what he did on tape. He'd never have confessed to anything. He would have baited and goaded you into attacking him," he said, pointing out the harsh truth.

"He'd have threatened to hurt me, and you would have reacted. You and I know both it's true." Drew warned him not to argue. "I knew Aniel's dark side, how to piss him off, how to grab his attention, how to calm him...because I've lived it. You never knew the dark side of him and I never wanted you to see it," he reasoned, hoping Rylee understood, even if he hadn't said a word yet.

"The real reason was I love you. All of you. This place is my home now, and the people who live here are my family," he admitted quietly. "I couldn't have lived with myself if I let Aniel get his eyes on even one of them. Because, if I failed, I knew what he would do to them, and he would make them suffer. I knew the pain he would inflict on them, and I'd rather go through it a thousand times than let someone else take my place."

Rylee sighed, ruffling his hair as he turned sideways to wrap Drew in his arms. "I love you, kitten. You're the most incredible man I've ever met," he whispered, unable to hide the thick emotion in his voice, the threatening of tears.

"I love you too. But you have to talk to me," he argued, unwilling to surrender.

"Okay." Taking a deep breath, Rylee pressed their foreheads together dand began to talk. Out came the hurt, the fear, the nightmares he'd kept secret, the what-ifs running through his mind a hundred times a day.

In return, Drew shared his own.

Because, now Aniel was caged and Sheffield's case was closed, Drew and Rylee were the ones who had to live with the fallout. They had watched Sheffield bask in the limelight of solving a disturbing domestic violence case. Endured the hours of questioning, the curious looks, and the media attention after Sheffield told them about the animal hairs and Aniel's delusional belief in "magical creatures". They had been there to see a group of cops sweep the house, one last time, and come up empty of anything cat related.

Aniel had put them through that. But he'd also been the scapegoat they desperately needed. His belief in wild animals turning into humans, and Rylee's testimony of their past relationship, satisfied Sheffield and his boss. They believed the fraternity had been framed by Aniel. Hairs planted. Witnesses bribed. Rumours circulated by Aniel himself. To discredit Rylee, hurt Drew, and put a wedge between them.

And, through it all, it barely touched the worst scars Aniel had left behind.

What they'd experienced would never be okay, but at least they could go through it together. They could *be* there for each other, *with* each other and to *heal* each other. Because, they were the ones who had to live knowing how hard they had to fight to escape a touch of danger.

Acknowledgements

Thank you to the entire team at NSP for making this such a smooth process. You all made me feel welcome and gave me the confidence to grow. I'm so happy to have my book in your capable hands.

Special thanks to my editor, Stacey Jo, who has taught me so much and made this entire editing process stress-free. This book is better because of you.

Thank you to all my readers on Wattpad, for encouraging me to tell this story. And all my followers on FB who stuck with me throughout the process from submission to publication.

Most of all, thank you to my parents, who support every book, every new venture, and listen to my complaints when the characters give me trouble.

About the Author

Elaine White is the author of multi-genre MM romance, celebrating 'love is love' and offering diversity in both genre and character within her stories.

Growing up in a small town and fighting cancer in her early teens taught her that life is short and dreams should be pursued. She lives vicariously through her independent, and often hellion characters, exploring all possibilities within the romantic universe.

The Winner of two Watty Awards – Collector's Dream (*An Unpredictable Life*) and Hidden Gem (*Faithfully*) – and an Honourable Mention in 2016's Rainbow Awards (*A Royal Craving*) Elaine is a self-professed geek, reading addict, and a romantic at heart.

Website: www.ellelainey.wixsite.com/author

Email: elainewhite.author@gmail.com

Facebook: www.facebook.com/elainewhite.author

Twitter: @ElleLainey

Also Available from NineStar Press

Connect with NineStar Press

www.ninestarpress.com

www.facebook.com/ninestarpress

www.facebook.com/groups/NineStarNiche

www.twitter.com/ninestarpress

www.tumblr.com/blog/ninestarpress

www.ingramcontent.com/pod-product-compliance
Lightning Source LLC
Chambersburg PA
CBHW062018190726

48284CB00012B/707